Bright Blue Planet creeps under your skin—and stays there. Compelling characters and moral challenges race along with a suspenseful plot. Leaves you wanting more!

—ZOE ROUTH, BEST-SELLING AUTHOR OF *THE OLYMPUS PROJECT*

An emotion-driven science fiction novel, *Bright Blue Planet* carries the best and worst of what we imagine for our future. As Catanzarite weaves a world of clones, aliens, and supreme leaders, she ultimately asks readers to consider what it means to be human.

—REBECCA M. ZORNOW, AUTHOR OF *DANGEROUS TO HEAL*

This story pulled me in right away, the pace fast and intriguing. Once again, author Kim Catanzarite has written a brilliant and captivating story.

—TRICIA T. LAROCHELLE, AUTHOR OF THE SARA BROWNE SERIES

PRAISE FOR THEY WILL BE COMING FOR US

They Will Be Coming for Us offers both quality writing and an irresistible story—a winning combination all around.

—BLUEINK REVIEW (STARRED REVIEW)

Well-constructed science fiction with an admirable heroine and a chilling premise.
—KIRKUS REVIEWS

The perfect melting pot of pace, plot, and problems . . . this tale is sure to keep readers turning the pages from cover to cover.
—READERS' FAVORITE (CONTEST WINNER)

Readers will bond strongly to Svetlana as she struggles to unravel the secrets of her new family in this sci-fi thriller.
—BOOKLIFE REVIEWS

PRAISE FOR JOVIAN SON

Depth and substance right down to the final startling and deeply heartfelt plot twist . . . [*Jovian Son* is] a supremely clever and emotional story that is not to be missed.
—THE PRAIRIES BOOK REVIEW

Evander is a fascinating secondary hero.
—JOHN M. MURRAY, CLARION REVIEWS

Kim Catanzarite excels in depicting changing family interactions and relationships against the backdrop of sci-fi events.
—DIANE DONOVAN, MIDWEST BOOK REVIEW

Jovian Son takes readers on a thrill ride.
—BLUEINK REVIEW

ALSO BY KIM CATANZARITE

BRIGHT BLUE PLANET

KIM CATANZARITE

forster
publishing
A LUCY H SOCIETY BOOK

ISBN: 978-1-7359522-5-3 (paperback)

ISBN: 978-1-7359522-4-6 (ebook)

Printed in the United States of America

1 3 5 7 9 10 8 6 4 2

Published by Lucy H Society Books, an imprint of Forster Publishing, United States of America. Distributed by Ingram Book Group, Ingramcontent.com.

Cover design by Damonza

❀ Created with Vellum

Jupe, this one's for you

"People fail to get along because they fear each other; they fear each other because they don't know each other; they don't know each other because they have not communicated with each other."

—Martin Luther King Jr.

BRIGHT
BLUE
PLANET

E vander was convinced he didn't need Elsa and Martin anymore.

It had been six months since he'd retired from the presidency, and every morning he and his secret service duo, a pair of AI-enhanced hybrids who followed him everywhere he went, rode to Starbright International headquarters together in a state-of-the-art self-driven van. He easily could have driven himself in an ordinary vehicle, but whenever he pointed this out, Elsa, the lead in said secret service duo, would glance at him with her too-blue crystalline eyes and say, "Your safety takes precedence, I'm afraid."

The government had its rules, and one of them was to provide protection for former presidents and their families, whether they wanted it or not. As a Jovian endowed with Jovian senses, Evander felt it was unnecessary.

Only six months ago, he, Nadia, and the two kids had left Washington, DC, and moved into a spacious Colonial home, newly refurbished from top to bottom, in Kirksberg, Pennsylvania, the same town in which his Russian mother, Svetlana, fell in love with and married his Jovian father, Andrew.

The neighborhood could not have been safer—or quieter.

Evander missed the Oval Office, and needless to say, the job he'd held for twelve years as the American president. He missed being busy every minute of the day and solving problems and getting heated about the injustices in the world. He missed the constant stream of challenges he had faced as the man in charge, the stirring speeches he made, and the travel and negotiations with Earth's leaders. Most of all, he missed making positive change for the greater good and keeping his finger on the pulse of the planet.

Not that he wouldn't do these things anymore, just not to the extent that he once had.

Evander had done his best to reacquaint himself with "normal" life, as far as that was possible for a past president and clandestine member of the Jovian elite. The American population knew him as the most-beloved leader the country ever had, and they assumed he was human through and through. He was actually a hybrid: the son of a human woman and the first Jovian man to produce an heir for the Jovian family.

Since he'd returned to a job at Starbright International, the family's aerospace company, Evander had headed a few noncrucial projects. He also attended many meetings with the potential to tackle serious topics, but they ended up going nowhere, not for lack of effort on his part.

The meeting scheduled for that morning would no doubt be more of the same. And that was only one of many things bothering him that day.

As soon as he entered his office, his cell rang. The display read "Home" and beside that, "Your Wife." Elsa had set up his contacts, and this is what she'd input for Nadia. He picked up, glad for a reason to join the meeting late. "Hey, honey."

"Daddy, do you know a man named James?"

The adorable and energetic voice on the other end of the

line belonged to his five-year-old daughter, Natasha. Every once in a while she experimented with her mother's cell phone.

Evander leaned against the edge of his black cherry desk and clicked View so he could be face-to-face with her full Russian cheeks and expressive gray-blue eyes, just like her mother's. "Daddy knows a lot of people, sweetheart," he said, "and, yes, some of them are named James."

"I had a dream last night." Strands of her fine hair fell into her eyes, and she pushed them away. "The nice man named James said he's coming to see us. I just wanted to tell you. He's been away for a long time, but he'll be here soon."

Uncle Jimmy? Evander had experienced a vague sense of Jimmy's presence earlier that morning as he viewed the sunrise. The prior weekend, Nadia had thrown Evander an intimate party for his fiftieth birthday (or the equivalent of fifty, as he aged at a progressive rate), and he'd remembered that his mother had given birth to him on her own birthday. Whenever thoughts led to Svetlana, they also led to eccentric Uncle Jimmy, the outcast of the Jovian family and the only one who'd shown Svetlana any compassion. Too bad Evander never knew the man outside of his mother's stories about him—the Jovian elite had banned Uncle Jimmy from Earth twenty-five years ago, when Evander was just a baby.

"It was only a dream, sweetie," he told Natasha. "How are you feeling today?"

"I want to go outside and play in the backyard, but I don't think Mommy wants me to. She gets mad when I ask. Can I please go outside?"

Frustration crinkled her button nose and flattened the curves of her still-babyish face. Natasha conveyed enough emotion for herself and her much-less-demonstrative older brother, Dmitri, who was eight.

"She's not angry with you at all, and of course you can go

outside. Take Eliot with you and don't run. The doctor says walking is fine." Eliot was one of the family's secret service agents. The one who liked kids.

"What about cartwheels?" she said.

"Hm. I'm not sure. How do *you* feel about cartwheels?"

"I think slow cartwheels are all right. Not fast ones."

"Okay," he said, "but just a few."

Evander's cheerfulness crumbled as he thought of the many cardiology tests Natasha had been put through and the second opinion they would obtain from the specialist the following day. The doctor who'd discovered the problem believed Natasha had inherited the heart defect that killed Andrew, Evander's Jovian father, at the age of thirty—but Evander couldn't accept that diagnosis for his little girl.

He tried hard not to let the sadness show when he smiled at her through the cell phone and said, "Take care of yourself, sweetheart. Remember, no running. And kiss Mommy for me. I'll be home in time for dinner."

"Bye-bye, Daddy."

He signed off, preoccupied with worry for his youngest child.

When he looked up from the blank screen, he found Elsa in front of him, her tall, lanky frame poised like a marble statue in the usual white pantsuit.

"You need to see this, sir," she said. "It's about Philadelphia."

She touched the paper-thin screen on the wall and an image flickered to life. Then her face became blank, her asymmetrical hairstyle cutting a sharp angle across the side of her head, as she used her connective capacity to pick up the right news clip.

The caption across the bottom of the screen read "Protests Turn Deadly at Liberty Square."

"It's a tragic day for all of us in Philadelphia," a female

newscaster said, standing at the outskirts of Independence Lawn. "No one could have predicted that a peaceful protest in support of clone and hybrid civil rights would become a tragic event. Behind me, you're seeing the aftermath of a horrible accident that left ten humans aged twenty to seventy-one deceased at the scene.

"The protest turned deadly when busloads of humans entered the venue with what appears to have been a violent agenda. No particular group has claimed responsibility, but authorities have begun a federal investigation. So far, there have been no arrests, and the fatalities have been deemed accidental."

Evander could not believe what he was hearing. Ten humans dead at a peaceful gathering of clones and their supporters? *How did this happen?*

Tensions had grown between the two races over the last dozen years—that much Evander admitted—but to this extent? He was aware that the introduction of clones and hybrids into society could have gotten off to a better start. While many humans accepted the new race, it was in large part because doing so benefitted them and the country as a whole. In a nation that had grown too violent for its own good, the clones and hybrids filled the many roles humans no longer wanted to fill—policing, soldiering, guarding— dangerous, life-risking positions that maintained public order and sometimes ended in premature death.

Due to their calm demeanor and superior strength, the clones proved well-suited to such roles, and humans welcomed them as protectors. But that was all. They didn't see them as equals. They saw them as a new genetically engi- neered race; they didn't know the clones' superiority actually came from Jovian DNA. And they didn't value them the way they valued what they considered "real" humans.

This became a problem recently when the clones began to

publicly express their desire for a better quality of life. They wanted to be able to pursue careers outside of protecting, vocations they naturally felt inclined to do, the jobs humans didn't want them to take. Perhaps even more important, they demanded equal standing in society. No more second-class citizenship and all the negativity that came with it.

For the past week, Evander had tried to set up an appearance at Independence Lawn. He wanted to lend his calming voice to the protests taking place, to act as a proponent of peace, but his successor in the White House, President Annalise Abela, insisted there was no need for him to get involved. Better to downplay the event, she'd said, speculating that the former president's presence would only shine a brighter light on the conflict between the two races.

He should have persuaded Abela to make an appearance herself.

On the screen, the newscaster with long strawberry-blonde hair stepped up to a woman standing with her hand on the shoulder of a boy of elementary school age. "You were here at the time of the incident?"

"Yes, that's right. Me and my son."

"Can you tell us what happened?" She held the mic in front of the woman.

"A small group of, I don't know, maybe seventy-five clones gathered early this morning, and at least that many humans came in support of them. They'd been meeting here, on the lawn, around the clock for about a week. Each day the crowds got larger, and there really hadn't been any problems. The clones and hybrids, most of them dressed in their black security uniforms, hung around in front of the amphitheater. Occasionally one of them climbed onstage and talked about their life and how second-class citizenship has prevented them from living the way they want to live. The humans for the most part listened respectfully."

The newscaster pulled the mic back to herself. "But all of that changed, didn't it?"

The woman nodded. "It did. Last night, the city brought in those long metal crowd-control fences that you see on the lawn's perimeter, to keep people corralled in the main area, you know, steering them away from the historic buildings that make up Liberty Square. At around 8 a.m., I think it was, a huge group of people arrived. They brought signs and loud music, and they were chanting, 'Clones Go Home,' you know, and things like that. It was *a lot* of people, a lot more than had showed up earlier in the week. Rumor had it most of them were bussed in from other parts of the country. The lawn started to get pretty crowded.

"My son's only eight, so we crossed to the far side, where there were less people and only a couple of barricades." She pointed across the way.

"It turned out to be a good thing you did," the newscaster said in a dire tone.

"Well, I could feel the tension growing," the woman replied. "You know, a lot of people don't support the clones or their civil rights agenda. The crowds funneling in gathered around the middle of the lawn for a short time, and then all at once, I heard a high-pitched whistle, and the group of them took off toward the amphitheater, where the clones were speaking. It was like they were in a race—they had no weapons, everyone is scanned on the way in—but they all started running at the same time, and I worried about the clones and their supporters." She pulled her son closer, resting her hands upon his shoulders.

"But the clones knew what to do in order to escape a mob like that," the newscaster said. "Security *is* their thing."

"Yes, and when they saw the mob coming, they scattered. A couple of them knocked down a segment of the metal fencing and led human supporters to safety. Others leaped onto the stage and lifted people up with them. But some were still on the lawn, and they became trapped by the rushing crowd. The screams we heard—" The woman's lips trembled, and she stopped speaking.

The newscaster leaned in. "It must have been awful. They simply couldn't get out of the way fast enough?"

The woman shook her head as she gathered herself, then cleared her throat. "It all happened very fast. The mob was like a giant train reeling off the tracks. People were knocked down and others, swept into the barriers. I wasn't even sure what was happening. My son and I stayed where we were, out of the way."

"It sounds a lot like a tsunami."

"It was. . . . That's what it was like. A human tsunami."

The newscaster tapped her earpiece. "Well, thank you for speaking with us. It's certainly a tragedy this country won't soon forget." Then, turning back to the camera, she said, "This is USN correspondent Susan Fitzpatrick coming to you from Independence Lawn in downtown Philadelphia. We'll report back as new updates on the situation emerge."

The volume lowered and then muted.

Evander didn't move. *Ten human beings dead.*

Elsa said, "Time for your meeting, sir."

He raised his hand. "I'm going to need a minute."

"Of course." She joined her counterpart, Martin, who stood at attention by the office door.

This could have been prevented. Evander had written the equal opportunities legislation that *should* have paved a way for clones and humans to get along. He'd offered to speak at an early protest, to set the tone and influence the crowd and the surrounding nation to take a peaceful path to coexistence, to move the clone's agenda gently forward toward an equal balance of power in the real world, not only on paper.

And yet he hadn't done it. Hadn't protected the humans *or*

the clones.

He thought back to the day his mother left this world for good, fifteen years prior, before he was elected president. Svetlana had entered a life pod on a spaceship among hundreds of other travelers journeying to various destinations in the solar system. She was headed to a universe in which Jovians didn't exist, a past universe where she and Andrew could live as two ordinary human beings, in peace.

Evander knew she wouldn't leave without his encouragement, so he had provided it. "Trust me," he'd said. "This world will not always be a good place for your kind."

But saying so only worried her. If the clones the Jovians created were more intelligent and superior in physical strength, she wondered what would become of the ordinary humans. Would the new humans dominate the old, and if so, what would that mean? If the strongest survive in this world, what would happen to the weak?

That day, Evander made her a promise, one he'd done his best to keep throughout his presidency, a promise he would continue to uphold for as long as he lived. "I'll take care of the ordinary humans as best I can," he'd told her, "no matter what happens. I give you my word."

And now, as predicted, the tension had come to a head between clones and humans in Philadelphia. The newer, stronger race threatened the older, less-dominant one—and the older one was prepared to fight in order to keep their position on top of the evolutionary ladder.

Philadelphia had become the epicenter of conflict that threatened a slow ripple of unrest throughout the rest of the world. None of the Jovian elite had listened when Evander warned them of the potentially fatal hostilities brewing below the surface of the planet he'd worked so tirelessly to save.

Well, maybe now they would.

2

The car needed charging. As Fran Vasquez drove the mini SUV to Starbright and pulled into his VIP parking space in the back of the building, the sun began to brighten the sky. Every bit of light would help; that is, if the solar panels on the car's roof weren't as dirty as his wife, Lisa, claimed they were.

As he exited his vehicle, he gazed into the woods just beyond the landscaped area and observed the tree with the remnants of the weather-worn platform he'd built into its branches long before he worked there. Years ago, prior to becoming an employee, he'd scoped out Starbright on a regular basis—at the time, he and Svetlana wrongly assumed they might be able to breach its telepathically monitored walls.

He often chuckled when he considered how shocked Svetlana would be that he ended up commanding Starbright's security squad for her Jovian in-laws.

Svetlana had been gone for almost fifteen years, and there wasn't a day he didn't wonder about her and his best buddy, Andrew. Had she made it back to him? Could it even be real, going back in time? Traveling to another universe? Sounded like a lot of mumbo-jumbo to him, and sometimes his practical brain did its best to rationalize away what he assumed to be true—but then he remembered that David, "the supreme being," once transformed into a force of energy of which Fran had never seen nor heard occurring on Earth. In an attempt to take Svetlana's son, David caused some kind of supernatural thunder storm, earthquake, magnetic field phenomenon—and he did it right in the middle of Kirksberg Park.

Not only that, David was the same "person" who, ten years later, used Jovian medicine to grow back the arm Fran had lost as an FBI agent in a live-fire training exercise. So, yeah, somehow that put the possibility of time travel into perspective for him. Crazy, mind-boggling perspective, but perspective nonetheless.

The Jovian elite had never known what to do with Svetlana. After she left this universe, the family acted the way they would have had she passed away: they planted a headstone next to Andrew's, arranged a short service for her, and placed a death notice in *The Kirksberg News*.

If Fran hadn't stood in the observation booth and watched Svetlana enter a life pod on that spaceship, he would have assumed they'd killed her. *Even if they are nonviolent people*, he told himself before blowing a forceful sigh through his lips.

But the family had treated Fran well. After David replaced his arm (and Fran realized he could trust the Jovians), they gave him a job in Starbright's security squad and began paying him a more-than-fair salary to do it. Now, fifteen years later, he headed up security for the Kirksberg location under the supervision of Leo, possibly the friendliest of Jovian family members.

And he liked his job; he enjoyed being at the helm of the

squad of fifty men and women, 20 percent of them human, 80 percent clone. Most clones worked in various forms of security because it suited their stoic personalities so well— some of them seemed to have no emotions whatsoever, which was good for an occupation where confrontation and violence occurred. Clones excelled at security forces, and they did it all in a surprisingly nonviolent way. They disarmed, and they didn't shoot except under dire circumstances of self-defense.

Fran paused in front of the ocular detection screen at the rear entrance, where everyone who worked security entered the building. Since the day he took over the squad, there was no more leaving doors unlocked and unguarded the way they used to be. No more relying on Jovian senses to know when someone entered the premises—or planned to make an attempt. Not that Fran assumed their telepathy was unreliable. It was as sharp as a blade, as far as he knew. But it wasn't public knowledge that Jovians were aliens with telepathic powers, and because Starbright conducted some government business via NASA (he wasn't sure how much), it had to at least *act* like a company with ordinary human powers.

The door popped open and the guard's usual "Morning, boss" arrived as expected.

"How's it going, Lenny?" Fran asked as he strode into the eerie-colored red room. The empty room glowed bright red every day of the week for no reason Fran knew except that Leo insisted it stay that way. Maybe the Jovians believed colored lights stunned the ill-intentioned into submission. On some level, they may have been correct about that, though Fran never asked to see the research behind it. Instead, he left it alone, which is what he often did when it came to Leo and the other Jovians, and the things they insisted upon. It was their building, after all, and he didn't want or need to know their secrets.

"You hear what happened in Philadelphia?" Lenny, a six-foot clone born of Leo's DNA, rarely chatted, but the latest news hit close to home, so Fran could see why he would be compelled to mention it.

"I did," Fran said, turning around to face him. He shook his head. "Awful news. What was it, ten people killed?"

Fran supposed all of the clones on the squad would have an opinion about what had happened, and he hoped it wouldn't cause tension between them. When the peaceful protests began in Philadelphia a few weeks ago, Fran wondered about his Starbright staff and whether the unrest would spill into the workplace. So far it had not.

"Uh-huh," Lenny said. "I heard both sides are bringing shit-tons of people back tonight."

"Really? Same venue? Seems like the city would shut it down."

"Nope, they're not going to. City police is run by clones. And the clones are the ones protesting, so I guess they can do whatever they want." Lenny grinned in an overly pleased manner that caused Fran to worry.

"So soon, with emotions running so hot?"

"Emotions are only running hot on one side," Lenny said, with a knowing look. Fran supposed he meant *your side.* Meaning, the human side, considering clones rarely became heated.

While clones and hybrids made up most security teams of all kinds, the managers of those teams—the bosses, captains, and commanders of those factions—remained, in most cases, human, so saying that the clones could "just do what they wanted" didn't make sense.

"Either way, seems wrong to gather there after the loss of so many lives," Fran said. "But I'm sure it's being handled."

Lenny shrugged. "Humans don't care if we die. I guess this just goes to show, we don't care if they do."

Fran stared at him for a second, surprised he'd said it out loud. "*I* care," he said, making sure Lenny got the message. "I care when *anybody* dies, whether they're 100 percent clone, 100 percent human, or anything in between."

"Oh, I know." Lenny stepped back to his place beside the door. "I know you do, but you're ..." he hesitated.

Fran widened his eyes and said, "Go on."

"You're not most people, that's all."

Unfortunately, Fran knew what he meant. When Evander took office and vowed to reduce the ridiculous number of violent acts committed in the country every year, many of the humans stepped away from careers in soldiering and security, and the clones stepped into them.

Problem was, the humans as a whole began to treat the clones and hybrids as if they were expendable. Those born of clone blood were easily identifiable—even the ones who came from marriages to humans. The Jovian DNA made them smarter, so they excelled in the school system, aced all of the mandated tests, and topped physical strength exams. Even if they tried to play dumb by failing the mental ability tests, their physical abilities could not be denied. And if you were a clone, hybrid, or any girl or guy with clone blood in the family, humans considered you less-than a natural human. Less than "real."

Suffice it to say, spilled clone blood became somehow less valuable than human blood—a lost clone, less devastating than the loss of a human. And that is how, in spite of the clones' superior intelligence and enhanced strength, they had nonetheless become second-class citizens.

The whole thing never failed to boggle Fran's mind.

"At Starbright, we're all equal members of the security squad, am I right?" he said.

"Yes, sir," Lenny said, snapping back into a security stance.

"Cool. I gotta get a move on. You have a good day."

"You too, Mr. Vasquez."

Clones like Lenny did their jobs well. They wouldn't let an incident like the one in Philadelphia affect their good judgment.

———

Thanks to the early hour, Fran encountered not a soul as he crossed the glamorous lobby with faceted windows, marble floors, and other finery he'd never get used to. Starbright was a strange place, no getting around it. He headed down the corridor, once again pausing in front of a door protected by eye recognition software. This one allowed him to enter the planetarium.

Caroline, or Queen Jovian (as he sometimes thought of her), had complained about a buzzing sound that she said, "just wasn't right." She worried about spying. Which was weird. Even for her.

She also mentioned something about interference, but Fran only pretended to know what she was talking about. He'd never claimed to be a tech guy.

He flicked on the lights. Without its moonlight and spray of stars lighting it up, the planetarium resembled the interior of an oversize eggshell: dull white walls with a cluster of chairs at its center. He moved into the middle of the room, put his hands on his hips, and stared up.

There it was. A light buzzing sound, not unpleasant. *She was right.* What could it be? The lights maybe? A loose electrical wire? Could her worry that someone had been spying on them be warranted? *Why here?*

He scratched his head as his gaze met with the circuit

panel across the room—he might have to call in an electrician for this one.

Just then, the door opened with an echoing bang that ricocheted off his chest. Out of habit, Fran bent at the knees and reached for his side holster, which he no longer carried. This wasn't the FBI and only under special circumstances did members of the security squad arm themselves with guns. He turned and recognized the skinny frame of his son, Max.

"Oh, man, this is cool." Max's enthusiasm soared to the high ceiling. "What's up, Dad? Sorry to startle you. Can I turn this thing on?"

Fran checked his watch. Seemed like a lot of energy for 7:45 a.m. "Didn't you work the late shift last night?"

Max had joined the security squad the prior week, an undertaking meant to fill the space between graduation from trade school and the start of his "real" career, whatever that would be.

"Yeah, so? I'm off today. You forgot? That's why I'm not in uniform."

"Why are you here, then? What am I forgetting?"

"I told you I wanted to check out this planetarium thing." He opened his arms wide and grinned at the ceiling. "You said Leo said Caroline okayed it."

"Oh, right. I just didn't think you'd be up this early."

Hard for Fran to believe, Max was in his twenties and still dreamed of becoming an astronaut. He'd graduated trade school with a two-year degree in avionics technology and hoped to start his career making repairs to spaceships—but those jobs were as few and far between as astronaut jobs.

The thing was, Max didn't know that the Jovians housed a spaceship in this very building, in the basement of Starbright —few humans did—and Fran would never tell him. Who knew what the kid might do with that information. He feared Max would volunteer to become a traveler, a thought that turned Fran's stomach. Travelers sometimes left the planet and never came back (Svetlana's birth parents, for instance). He couldn't let that happen to Max. His wife, Lisa, already made it clear that she'd kill Fran if that happened.

Fran needed Max to stay on Earth where he and Lisa could watch him and guide him, and make sure he didn't do anything too stupid.

"You've been dragging your ass lately," Fran said, back to studying the ceiling. "I assumed you'd want to sleep in."

For some time now, the kid had been "mildly depressed," or that's how Lisa diagnosed him. He needed a job to get out of bed for, something to keep busy with. And Fran needed another human on the security squad, so, as much as he hated the idea of Max hanging around Starbright, he'd given him the position. Temporarily. As a sort of internship. He figured a few months working at Starbright wouldn't be long enough for Max to get chummy with the Jovian elite or to learn their bigger secrets.

"Are you kidding? I'm lucky I have access to this place. I want to learn everything I can while I'm here. I mean, we're standing in a frickin' planetarium! Did you know there's a greenhouse on the property? I heard they have a collection of plants from outer space."

"Yeah, yeah, I know. Of course I know. I run security around here. Did you know *that*?"

Sometimes he couldn't hold back the sarcasm. It was something Lisa had him working on. Wasn't doing a great job of it, though.

The kid hadn't displayed this level of excitement about anything in years. Ever since he'd graduated trade school, he'd been under the weather, hunkering down in his room, skipping meals and sneaking bags of chips and cookies for dinner. He often wore his robe from morning till night. It used to be white; now it was an antique shade of dirty.

KIM CATANZARITE

Figures the one thing Fran didn't want him to be too interested in was the one thing he obsessed over.

Max's shoulders drooped along with his verve. "What's your deal, Dad? Are you telling me you don't think this place is cool?"

Fran didn't want to ruin his fun. If he loved astronomy and spaceship stuff, so be it. Fran had listened to all the astronomical facts he could stand back when he was an undergrad with Andrew Jovian, when they roomed together and became best buds. Thanks to Andrew, he'd learned more about the cosmos than he ever wanted to know—the guy spent half his life staring through a telescope.

"Yeah, it's cool," Fran said. "Sorry, it just gets old hat after a while."

"Old hat?" The kid beamed a snarky smile. "Did you just say 'old hat'?"

"It's a saying," Fran muttered. Turning fifty-six a few weeks prior had dampened his spirits, and sometimes Fran caught himself using old-man jargon.

Max never missed an opportunity to remind him how uncool he was. "Yeah, for octogenarians maybe," he said. Then he rubbed his hands together as if anticipating a tasty meal. "So, when can I turn this thing on and watch the sky light up?"

Fran rolled his eyes. "Fine. I'll sweep the place for bugs when you're done."

"Sweep for bugs? From outer space?" Max's face lit with the prospect.

Fran stared at him, no comment.

"You mean a different kind of bug," Max said. "But who'd want to spy in here?"

"I'll explain later, just get the remote."

3

E vander entered the conference room prepared for a serious discussion centered on the tragedy that had occurred a few hours earlier, in Philadelphia.

The others had arrived before him, and all except Miranda, who currently handed out paper tablets, were settled in their seats. Present today were not only Caroline, the matriarch of the Jovian family, and Miranda (Caroline's right hand) but also Aunt Constance (the lead scientist) and Leo (in charge of security). David (the one they called "supreme being") had been missing from meetings two weeks in a row due to what Caroline referred to as a "special assignment."

Edmund, the patriarch of the family would not be present, either. He had left Kirksberg for Io, Jupiter's inhabitable moon, soon after Evander retired from the presidency. According to Caroline, some problem with the oneness—the family's internal communication system that made available all Jovian thoughts and experiences—was preventing Edmund from touching base. The oneness had never failed before, so not being able to use it to contact his grandfather caused Evander some concern, though none of the other Jovians seemed bothered by it.

Evander took his place seated across from Caroline, who occupied the table's head, a clear demarcation of the division of power and hierarchy of rank.

"Good morning, everyone," he began, pulling in his chair and putting on his game face. "Grandmother, if I may be so bold as to suggest we discuss the situation in Philadelphia. I believe it warrants our immediate attention, as ten humans have perish—"

"Miranda will begin the meeting with an update on the Mars program," Caroline interrupted, "which I'm pleased to say is up and running as of this morning."

Humans had been trying to launch a manned spaceship to Mars since the 1970s. A couple of weeks ago, Caroline agreed it was a good idea to help them, and she gave the go-ahead to fast-track a program that would not only assist NASA in the space flight but also guide them to colonization. Miranda headed up the project.

Why that would take precedence over a tragedy that occurred that very morning in their own backyard, Evander did not know.

Miranda, a petite woman with clean-cut girl-next-door features, gave the appearance of country affability, which is why she had been the perfect Jovian to trick Svetlana into friendship. Back then, Svetlana was having a baby (him) and the Jovians needed to manipulate her into staying close to them. So Miranda had stepped into a Southern accent and a pair of jeans, and put her neighborly baking skills and pretend kindheartedness to good use—too bad all of it had been a cover for her cold-hearted ambition. She'd proved pivotal in the plan to keep Svetlana and newborn Evander under lock and key at Chateau L'Origine. For this reason and others, Evander had never liked her.

Miranda stood, beginning her presentation with a flash of her blue eyes and an arrogant smile in Evander's direction, imparting the message, "My project is more important than your news."

Evander tried to see into Aunt Constance's thoughts, and then Leo's—*surely they had to care about a fatal conflict between clones and humans*—but he only hit a wall. He couldn't hear either of them.

This may or may not have been intentional, or even reason for concern. Perhaps whatever the problem was with the oneness wasn't his grandfather's alone. Edmund, far away, was unreachable, but right now Evander couldn't reach two people directly in front of him, either. A week ago, he had expressed his concern to Caroline, and she came back with her usual, "Nothing to worry about" answer. The equivalent of a shrug, one that did little to set Evander's mind at ease. He'd never been unable to reach his grandfather—or anyone else in the family—and sensed something brewing below Caroline's offhand reassurances.

Then again it was impossible for mere Jovian mortals like himself to surmise what his grandmother was thinking. She was so powerful, there was no breaking into thoughts she didn't want him to hear, not even when this feeling of something "off" wouldn't let him be.

The paper tablets Miranda had passed out at the start of the meeting lit up with details of the Mars program, displaying photos of the various regions of the red planet as she spoke of the reconnaissance orbiters and their findings.

None of it was news to Evander—or any of the other Jovian elite, no doubt—and instead of giving Miranda his attention, Evander lingered on the problem with the oneness. When he was honest with himself, he considered the possibility that whatever was wrong, might be *his* problem alone.

After all, in the past month or so, Evander had noticed a waning in his connection to the Jovian oneness as a whole. The trouble had begun as a subtle dampening of chatter within his mind, as if someone had turned down the volume. He'd denied it at first. But as the weeks passed, even the loudest of voices he normally heard (those of Caroline, David, Constance) had softened, dulled, become less easy to decipher. At times he feared he was going deaf to the family altogether.

He didn't bring up the problem to Caroline in any specific way because he didn't want her to know. She'd grown cooler toward him since Edmund had left for Io. She'd always been cold to the rest of the world, but not to him. He was "the grandson she'd always wanted." For him, she held a special place. A fondness she didn't extend the others. An attentiveness. When he was a child growing up with his mother in Russia, Caroline spoke to him in his mind most evenings, telling him to take care of himself and to use his time wisely. She told him he was special and powerful. Irreplaceable. She made sure he knew he remained in her thoughts and that she wanted only the best for him.

His mother had not known about these communications. Svetlana had been part of the Jovian oneness, but only so much as a human mind can be. The messages she received came in the form of foggy images and blunt, long-lasting headaches. Many times Evander had wanted to tell Svetlana how the oneness worked. How every Jovian possessed two consciousnesses—one, a private, solitary mind much like a human consciousness, and the other, a higher-level consciousness in which one could tap into the thoughts and experiences of all other Jovians at will. This was the oneness.

It was possible to be a Jovian and exist like humans do, with nothing but your own thoughts. And if you were skilled —and all of the Jovian elite were—you could keep that consciousness mostly to yourself. Evander often kept his thoughts to himself (though Caroline and David could get in if they wanted to). He liked privacy. And he liked feeling human. It came naturally to him, though he readily admitted that the second consciousness came in handy as well.

He never shared any of this with Svetlana because she already hated the way the Jovians meddled in their lives. He couldn't let her know that he and Caroline spoke daily, that any Jovian anywhere could speak to him at any time, and that moving to Russia to escape the family had made little difference when it came to that connection.

Caroline had been an attentive grandparent throughout his short childhood and that attentiveness had extended throughout his presidency. But now that he'd returned to Kirksberg, she treated him like the less-powerful, less-knowing grandson he was, nothing more, as if he weren't a former commander in chief and the first president the country's people loved dearly enough to change the Constitution in order that he could serve a third term.

Then again, the position held only so much weight with Caroline, considering her rank in the galaxy.

Finally Miranda wrapped up her overly detailed Mars program report.

"Thank you for that, Miranda," Caroline said, and with abrupt assertiveness, she added, "This meeting is over."

Evander made a move to argue, but before he could, Caroline uttered, "Evander, please stay."

So she wants to talk after all, he thought. *Finally.*

While the other Jovians filed out of the conference room, Caroline gestured for Evander to take the seat beside hers. Only the Miranda clone, the one named Randa, stayed behind like a sentry at the door, reminding Evander that Caroline didn't wholly trust him. Meanwhile Elsa and Martin remained outside of the room, where Caroline insisted they stay. She'd never trusted the government's secret service, either.

As he sat beside her, an unexpected swell of intimidation settled upon him like the vague start of a sore throat. It would have been nice to know what she was thinking, to be mentally attuned, but hardly a murmur from the collective Jovian community came through the oneness at the moment, let alone Caroline's normally clear-as-a-bell voice.

What is wrong with me? he wondered.

Caroline sat perfectly still with hands clasped and resting in her lap, her cheeks colored in an elegant hue and blonde bob sharply clipped. The golden glow from her satin blouse was enough to make a human squint. "You have played your part as a world leader very well," she said, "and I'm glad you've had some time to spend at home, but we need you elsewhere."

He'd been sitting back in his chair in an attempt to appear casual, but this statement stiffened his spine and made him lean in. "Elsewhere as in?"

"Oh, I don't know. Mintaka maybe," she said as if she hadn't given it a thought. "Or perhaps you'd like to join Edmund on Io?"

He raised his brows. "You've heard from him?"

"No, no one has," she said, and she pointed at Randa, who approached the bookshelf and pulled from its midst a weighty-looking tome. The clone, petite like Miranda but with a stiffer gait, walked over and handed the book to Caroline.

Evander glimpsed the title: *Electromagnetic Compatibility.* Why she needed that, he could only guess.

More important, why would Edmund need him on Io? If

he did, wouldn't he have arranged for it months ago, before he'd left? And Mintaka seemed an even stranger suggestion. Mintaka was the place for creators like quirky Uncle Jimmy. But Evander wasn't a creator. He was a leader, one who wrangled mobs and convinced entire nations to get with the program. During his presidency, he'd influenced both humans and clones to take action for the good of the planet, for the survival of their species and all living things. His talents lay in getting the masses to drive electric cars and disabling the toxicity of the Net and convincing those who once ate fast-food to switch to an organic (or better yet, vegan) diet. He still couldn't believe how hard it had been to accomplish those things. But he'd gotten them done. Of course he'd gotten them done.

He wouldn't be able to do much influencing from Mintaka or Io—or anywhere else in outer space. The fact that Caroline suggested he go there made him wonder if there was some problem with the Moon Children, though something told him now was not the time to inquire about that.

Even if Edmund needed him on Io, his wife, Nadia, who'd grown up in a village in Russia, would never agree to raising the kids anywhere outside of Earth. Especially after what they'd learned about their five-year-old, Natasha, and her heart. . . . And now that he'd remembered Natasha's diagnosis, he had to will himself back to the conversation at hand.

"Do you want me to go to Mintaka or Io, or do you simply want me to get out of the way of the family's plans?" he said, minus the heat of accusation that gathered in his chest.

"Not at all. You proved to be an excellent president, just like I knew you would. You brought the planet back to a healthy, thriving state. You have fulfilled your familial duties. What happens next simply isn't your responsibility."

"What *is* happening next?"

She hesitated to respond, then tilted her head as if suspicious that he may be joking. "You're Jovian. You know the answer to that as well as I do."

But he didn't. As much as he didn't want to admit it to her, he couldn't see the way forward. The Jovian oneness had taken him only so far and then faded. At this point, he feared he would wake up one morning and find it altogether gone. And then what would he do? Would his life be adrift without it?

"Actually, I've been receiving mixed signals," he said, downplaying the problem and keeping the worry out of his voice. "Please tell me what's happening next."

She turned away and gazed out the window. "You saved the planet. That's why you were born. You've done your job."

Is she serious?

"Done, as in, forever? Is that what you're saying? And now you want me to leave?"

"You can be proud of yourself," she said. "There's a new president. She's perfectly capable. You made that happen, too."

Actually, Caroline had made that happen, though Evander did think highly of Annalise Abela, a full-blown civil rights advocate. Caroline had basically ordered him to help Abela win the last election, and he'd used his powers of influence to make it happen because her ideology matched his own to a large degree; granted, she'd been ineffective when it came to the recent situation in Philadelphia.

Since Evander had returned to Kirksberg, conversations with Caroline left him feeling more human than ever. It was no wonder his mother couldn't stand her. Part of him brightened remembering how often Svetlana had stood up to Caroline. How she referred to her as "The queen of no sense of humor."

"Speaking of Mintaka," he said, in a tone meant to lighten spirits, "I sense James is back on Earth. Is he here to visit you, specifically?"

Caroline blinked—her equivalent of leveling a look of surprise in his direction.

"You didn't know he was coming." He did his best *not* to appear smug. "So maybe I'm not the only one who hasn't been receiving all the family news?"

"If you were having problems with the oneness, you should have mentioned it," she said.

Should he tell her the truth about what he feared? He glanced away. "I worried it may have been done deliberately."

"Of course not," she said without hesitation. "I'll make sure David is aware."

"Thank you. And the three of us need to talk about what's happening in Philadelphia. President Abela doesn't think it's necessary for me to be involved, but after the incident this morning—"

"Your laws are taking care of it," Caroline said, without so much as furrowing her brow. "Your legislation is in place. I agree with President Abela."

"You are aware that my equal rights legislation isn't foolproof?" he said. "It sets a standard. It doesn't actually control minds and actions."

"What's happening is evolution," she said without pause. "And I understand why that might bother you—"

Bother me? "It's not only because my wife is human, Grandmother. My children possess very human traits, as you know, even if they are genetically part of this family. Not all Jovians are powerful and perfect."

At that, Caroline raised her chin. She wasn't quite as proud of her great-grandchildren as she was of him. Too much human in them for her tastes, he assumed.

"My mother was human, as you well know," he said, "and

when we sent her out of this world, I gave her my word that I'd protect the human species as best I can."

Caroline made no effort to respond. Her blank face plunged into a state of absolute boredom. Eager for him to have his say and leave, he was pretty sure.

"I keep my promises," he said, pushing back from the table.

"I remember that promise," she said. "And I don't think you should have made it." At that, she eyed Randa, who moved to open the door. "I understand your loyalty to the human race. Loyalty is a wonderful quality to have. Loyalty to one's extended family, for instance."

She *didn't* understand. That much was clear. She didn't have the capacity to understand because she was Jovian through and through. All of the Jovian elite lacked the empathy inherent in humans—and she was the queen.

He sometimes wondered what she looked like in her true form. He'd seen Jovians on Io and Europa, their sleek black bodies, shiny and smooth, with long, lean limbs and barely decipherable facial features. He wondered how tall she would be. Her personality made it easy to picture a body the height of a high-rise.

"I'll look forward to our next meeting," she said, without the smile most people put on with that phrase.

He paused there, met her empty gaze, and once again tried to read her. But he found nothing there, nothing to see or feel. "Thank you," he answered out of politeness.

He exited the room and sensed Elsa and Martin at his heels. "I'll need a minute," he told them as he headed into his office a couple of doors down, destined for the bathroom, the one place he could get away from the rest of the world, if only for a moment.

4

D own the corridor, someone shouted, "Hey, no! I didn't mean—stop!" Sounded like Max's voice. High-pitched in a panic.

The whine of a chair against floor tiles followed.

A scuffle in the break room?

Fran ran the rest of the way down the hall. He arrived to the thud of a punch making contact and his son thrown sideways before bouncing across the floor like tossed dice. The kid shot up with fire in his eyes, his hand dabbing a bloody lip and chest heaving.

Ten or twelve security squad employees stood by, mouths closed.

Fran couldn't tell which one of them had thrown the punch.

Max dropped into a chair, head bowed.

It took every cell in Fran's body to keep his voice to a low roar. "What the hell is going on here?"

Consuela spoke first: "Just a disagreement, sir. Between Leonard and, uh, Max."

"Why is my son bleeding?" He pushed past Consuela and

Andre, and stopped in front of Max, who continued to stare at the ground, hunched forward in a humiliated way.

"Somebody better start talking," Fran said.

Leonard, the highest ranking in the squad, stepped out of the circle of uniform-clad employees. Diligent, careful, mature, Leonard was at least a foot taller than Max. Fifty pounds more solid too. One of the early clones, he'd received his DNA from Leo, Fran's boss—his sandy hair, pale skin, and slate-gray eyes made that much obvious. He would have had a normal American-guy build, like Leo's, had he not spent the past two decades eating egg whites and lifting barbells in his free time.

Leonard stepped forward and said, "He was complaining about the job, sir."

"And?"

"We don't do that at Starbright."

"Okay. So, I don't understand," Fran said. "You *hit* him?"

"Yes, sir." Leonard perfected his already snapped-to soldier's stance: chest puffed to barrel size, boots together, arms straight as fence posts. The guy was a senior officer. It didn't make sense that he would throw a punch—or even slap someone.

Jovians never resort to violence.

"Everyone but Leonard and Max get out of here," Fran said. "Go find something to do."

"Yes, sir," they responded in unison before scattering like billiard balls.

Fran lingered on the fact that no Starbright employee on record had ever hit another employee. Period. Not even accidentally . . . or in self-defense. If a threatening individual accosted you, you were to take them to the ground and apprehend them using forceful but nonviolent measures. That's the way it was, the way it always had been as far as the Jovians were concerned.

How does Max always find a way to screw up?

Fran rubbed his forehead as he unearthed the commanding attitude he once saved for cocky FBI recruits. "You just punched your boss's kid, Leonard, so I'm gonna need to see you in my office immediately."

Leonard shook his head, his chin looking more square than usual. "You're not my boss, sir."

This gave Fran's face a reason to contort in a befuddled and infuriated way. "Excuse me?"

"Sir, you're not my—"

"You better believe I am," Fran said, determined not to hear the statement twice. "I've been your boss for the past eight years."

"I take orders from the Jovians—"

"What's gotten into you?" Spit flew from Fran's mouth. He pointed to the room's exit. "Get to my office before you say something really stupid."

The clone turned and left without another word.

Fran stared after him, perplexed. Clones were obedient. Difficult to rile. They had a shallow depth of emotion perfectly suited for this line of work. No one wanted their security staff punching, shooting, or otherwise going off because they were spooked, afraid, or angry. So how did Leonard end up so pissed that he broke rule number one and hit Max?

Max remained boneless in the chair, staring at the ground.

"What happened?" Fran said. "Hey, look at me."

The kid raised his head and blinked through his timidness. "He punched me in the mouth." A finger of blood from his lip wound around his chin. "He just admitted it. I didn't do anything."

"Right, but this group doesn't hit. What made him want to hit you?"

Max seemed to suffer a loss of words. All kinds of excuses usually gushed past his lips, so this was strange.

Maybe the kid is just scared. After all, Fran was standing with his hands on his hips the way angry bosses do. He softened his shoulders in spite of the agitation that pulled taut the ropes of his neck and settled into his ears. "Talk to me, Max."

"All I said was that I was still tired from working the late shift earlier in the week."

Fran felt his face scrunch with disbelief. "That's it?"

"Yup, that's it." Max looked up, hopeful.

It didn't seem right. One complaint from Max was enough to set Leonard off?

Fran blamed himself. He shouldn't have hired Max for this so-called internship. Lisa insisted it would be good for him, "just what he needed," a way out of his slump. And now look what had happened. Fran exhaled loudly through his nose. Nothing he could do about it except try to find a smooth way out.

"Okay," he muttered. "I've gotta go deal with this."

"What are you gonna do, fire him?" Max asked in an assuming way that raised Fran's blood pressure.

"He's worked here twenty years. He's a stellar employee. So, no, I'm not firing him."

"But he hit me." Max's bottom lip protruded in an infuriating manner. "He hit the boss's kid. He *should* be fired."

Fran scowled. "It's a swollen lip. Certainly not something I want to risk war over."

"It's one guy who punched me in the face because he didn't like my attitude," Max grumbled, "not a war."

His attitude? Now they were getting somewhere.

Fran tilted his head. "What attitude, exactly?"

"Nothing. *None*, I mean." Max resumed his study of the floor.

"Max," Fran said in a low growl, "if you don't tell me what—"

"He said I was a sad sack." The words raced out of Max's mouth. "Said my generation has had it too easy, that we're soft. Entitled. You know how much I hate that word."

And yet, Leonard isn't wrong.

"How long has this been brewing? I mean, crap, you only started the job last week. I told you to come to me if you ever had a problem. You can't give your co-workers attitude. They're basically soldiers. Each one of them. Just because they're nonviolent doesn't mean they won't—" He stopped. It was like explaining safety to a child. He closed his eyes and did his best to conjure calm. *Never should have agreed to hire him, but Lisa kept saying the kid needed to learn responsibility.* Fran raked his hand over his buzz cut.

Max slouched in the chair. "So you're thinking about firing me, then? I got hit, and you're firing me?"

"No one's getting fired," he said, sternly. "But it's not that simple. Leonard's a clone, and he has clone friends, and I don't know if you've noticed but 80 percent of the security squad is made up of clones. This department has to get along both in the office and out in the field. Otherwise we can't do our jobs. And you've seen what's happening in Philadelphia, I'm sure."

Max exhaled as if *he* were out of patience. "Just have Caroline deal with it."

For a fraction of a second, Fran considered it. But then his grownup self woke the hell up and remembered that if Caroline had to deal with it, she would think he had *failed* to deal with it. She would assume that he wasn't doing his job as her head of security. Or, at least, that he wasn't doing it well. The Jovians maintained zero tolerance for violence, so if Caroline discovered that one member of the security team had punched another, Fran didn't know what she'd do or how big a deal it would become. No, Caroline wasn't the answer. Maybe he could discuss it with Leo, or—Why the hell was he considering the kid's advice?

He jerked his pants up as he took a deep breath. "I'm going to handle it," he said, loud and clear. "Don't worry."

None of the royalty needs to know, he thought.

"In the fifteen years I've worked here, I never had a problem like this. Not till you joined the team," he muttered, diverting some of his own stress. He wanted to say more but stopped himself, knowing that if he did, Max might end up at home, hiding in his room, wearing his robe for another six months—and no one wanted that.

Max pulled his cell from his pocket and thumbed the screen. "It wasn't my fault," he said softly.

"Yeah, we'll talk about it at home."

5

Evander exited the staircase and turned left into the narrow corridor. Not many people visited this part of the facility aside from the botanist, a very old native Peruvian named Dayana. In all of the times he'd climbed the stairs to the greenhouse, he'd never met her.

Elsa led the way with Martin following two steps behind, as usual. Martin, a tall, thin man with close-cropped hair as dark as the smart black suit he wore daily, resembled in some ways a shadow. Very much a number-two guy, he left all of the talking to Elsa, speaking only when prompted. Lately when they moved through the halls in this way, with Elsa in front and Martin behind him, Evander felt as trapped as the middle of a sandwich, his inability to move about freely sticking uncomfortably to his sides. But he knew his limits, and foiling two highly trained government hybrids who were more AI than human at this point was never going to happen.

When they reached the entry to the greenhouse, Elsa stepped aside while Evander flashed his eyes in front of the ocular detection screen. Then she stepped in front of him, as did Martin, and began to clear the room.

A natural calm fell over Evander whenever he entered the warmth of the greenhouse. Located on the third floor, the glass panels rose from a quarter of the way up the wall and continued to the roof's apex. The humid interior smelled of peat moss with a subtle whiff of ammonia. The scent brought him back to the day he'd first arrived at Starbright—he'd been only ten years old, the equivalent of a nineteen- or twenty-year-old human—and Edmund had taken him on a tour of the facility. While Evander observed the hothouse for the first time, Edmund explained in succinct detail Evander's duty to the family. "You will be the first family president," he'd said with a gleam in his eye.

Edmund's words had filled him with the excitement that comes with embarking on an amazing adventure, one that would begin with a trip to Jupiter, or more specifically Io, home of Jovians and the Moon Children. While he was there, he'd learn all about outer space, the solar system, the galaxy in which they lived, and, of course, the Jovian heritage. Upon their return to Earth, Evander would be at the front of a senatorial campaign the Jovians used to set his course for the US presidency.

It was during this conversation that Evander decided Svetlana had been wrong about the Jovian side of the family. He understood why she wouldn't trust them, but at the same time, he *did* trust them. He believed their desire to do good in the world was genuine. He believed the family truly wished to guide the human race in doing away with violence and pollution and the many problems weighing the planet down. Young Evander wanted to work with them. He wanted to fulfill his role as a Jovian.

And now that he had accomplished all he set out to do for the family, he realized that Edmund had been right: his life to this point had been an amazing adventure. *Was it coming to an end so soon?* According to Caroline, he was to leave his home. The planet he'd granted years of service.

Elsa returned from clearing the area. "He's here," she said, as she and Martin took their places outside the entry door.

A shadow of movement beyond the section of exotic conifers drew Evander's attention. "Uncle Jimmy? Is that you?"

Jimmy was his biological grandfather, but Evander often forgot that. To him, Caroline was his grandmother and therefore Edmund, her husband, was his grandfather. Those were the roles they played, and that's what had been impressed upon him. But it was Jimmy who'd secretly provided the sample that penetrated Caroline's ovum and grew, in test tube form, into the child that would become Evander's father, Andrew.

Uncle Jimmy came out from behind a table of two-foot watery-blue pines that may have originated on Earth or Io. He held a small pinecone in his hand. "Evander the Mighty," he said, with a grin. "I see that the rumors are true. Svetlana and Andrew's marvelous child has grown into a marvelous young man."

"Young?" Evander laughed. "I've aged the equivalent of at least fifty human years, not too young by Earth's standards. It's good to see you looking so well, Uncle."

Jimmy opened his arms for a hug, and Evander obliged, noticing the pulpy feel of the older man's muscles, the delicate body of a plump seventy-year-old. Not the brain, however. Evander sensed a flurry of activity inside Jimmy's head similar to the thrum electric bees would make in a metal hive.

Uncle Jimmy's outward appearance didn't give the impression of a major player in the Jovian family, let alone the universe. With his messy, mostly bald crown, oversize belly, and baggy clothing, he was very much the absent-minded professor of the family, and definitely a rogue player. Jimmy lived in his own world and did things for his own reasons. He was the kind who didn't care for rules and often disregarded them. Sometimes Evander considered the possibility that he worked for a higher power—or *was* one, himself. No one, as far as Evander could tell, knew for sure.

"Compared to me, you're a baby." Jimmy tossed the little pinecone into the air and caught it.

"Yes, I guess you're right." Evander stepped back and leaned into the table behind him. "So, you're here. On Earth. What transformations should I expect to take place?"

It was well-known among Jovians that Uncle Jimmy acted like a catalyst for change for the human race. If you went back to any point in Earth's history during which a major invention affected the human landscape—the light bulb, for instance, or the telephone, the first computer—you would find Uncle Jimmy there, working behind the scenes. He "happened" to know some famous human beings, like Albert Einstein, Marie Curie, and Alan Turing.

Uncle Jimmy bent toward a purple flower on a vine and took a whiff. "Who me? I'm just here to do a little gardening."

Evander wondered if there was some underlying meaning in that statement. If so, it went over his head. But there were other topics of conversation he needed to address, so he let it float away. "I'm sure you're aware of what's going on with the humans in Philadelphia?" Evander asked.

Jimmy pulled some dried leaves from the plants to his left, then began to pluck the dead blossoms from a tray to his right. Without looking up, he said, "The human beings are doing fine as far as I can tell."

That was a disappointing statement if ever Evander heard one. "They may be on the cusp of warring with the clones you created," he said. "Something needs to be done."

Uncle Jimmy removed his focus from the flowers and met Evander's gaze. A gentle innocence settled over his face. "I've never made a human clone. I was against making the clones from the very beginning."

"And yet somehow, with your help, an entire race of them lives on this planet. How is that, I wonder, and please don't tell me it was written in the stars. Things like cloning don't just happen."

"Cloning was always sewn into the tapestry of human fate, even if that's not what you want to hear," he said, his cheeks pinkening. "You seem upset, are you?"

"I don't know. Maybe."

Jimmy went back to tending to the various plants. "You're human. It's to be expected."

"Yes, you're right. I'm human and I'm Jovian and I have emotions. From what I've been told, you experience them, too. Is that correct?"

Jimmy gave up on gardening and stepped up to Evander, tilting his head in a contemplative way. "I feel empathy. Empathy and all that comes with it."

"So you can understand when I tell you that I made a promise to my mother to protect the human race, and I intend to follow through because *she* means a lot to me."

"But you've already followed through. You've protected them with your legislation. You saved their planet, made it inhabitable again, safe again. I suspect you've done more for the humans than any other individual ever has . . . or will, for that matter." He paused before placing a heavy hand upon Evander's shoulder. "Your mother would be proud of you."

"That may be so, but what's happening in Philadelphia would concern her nonetheless," Evander said, stepping aside so he could get out from under Jimmy's hand. "I thought you cared about my mother. She always spoke so highly of you."

Jimmy blinked as if some dust had fallen into his eye. "I

care for her just as I care for you." He rubbed the back of his head, leaving a thin veil of hair circling in a whirl. "And, for your information, it was Aunt Constance who came up with the science that led to cloning. I only shared some notes. Either way, it had to be done in order for other occurrences to . . . occur."

"In spite of that," Evander said, "the humans and clones are at odds. The humans are the physically weaker beings, and they know it. They've been fearful of the clones from the start. The only leg they have to stand on is a societal one. They are purebred. 'Real,' as they like to say. But they're not stupid. They know the clones are smarter and stronger, and therefore destined to replace them."

"What you describe may be an issue now," Uncle Jimmy said with optimistic light in his eyes, "but it won't always be. Minds will change. In time, all of the genes will have mixed. There will be no such thing as a purebred human. No reals or fakes, clones or hybrids. Only humans with varying degrees of Jovian DNA. That's the beauty of it."

Uncle Jimmy argued with ease and self-assurance, but Evander knew it wasn't that simple. Life never was. Humans, in particular, never were. "Twelve years ago, if the people had known I was a hybrid," he said, "if they knew what Jovians were and that I actually am one—and let's hope they never find out—I would not have been elected."

"I believe you're right about that." Uncle Jimmy guided an apricot-colored tulip blossom under his nose and took a whiff. "The humans didn't know what a hybrid was when you were first elected. They wouldn't have trusted you."

"The day the government 'admitted' to hosting the so-called Clone Development Program," Evander went on, "which you and I both know they never agreed to, humans knew for sure that genetically engineered clones had entered the population. They also assumed the clones were made for military purposes. How else could the government explain it away? They certainly couldn't admit that a wealthy family in Pennsylvania had cloned the species without their blessing."

"So it worked out for the best," Jimmy said, as if all was well in the world.

"Except that now there are two kinds of humans, and one is stronger than the other."

Uncle Jimmy made a face to indicate this was no big thing. "It's a mere wrinkle that will work itself out. Humans will surprise you. They always surprise me."

He continued through the maze of potting tables, and Evander followed, stopping in front of an aquarium filled with aquatic plants from Europa, some strange, eel-like things Evander never much liked.

"That's very charming," Evander said, "but in Philadelphia the two factions are a step away from declaring war." He wore his game face, determined not to back down. He needed Jimmy in his corner. Especially if Caroline remained steadfast in her plan to do nothing. "I'm no longer in office. I no longer have the power to deal hands-on with the situation. Someone has to do something before more violence breaks out. If it does, Philadelphia will be the lit match that starts a global inferno."

Jimmy turned away from the plants, his concern making stone of his face. "Violence? The clones are Jovian, and the Jovians are a nonviolent people."

Evander shrugged. "So far they have been."

"What is your specific concern?"

"Several human beings died at a protest last night. Accidental deaths, yes, but the animosity between humans and clones has become heated. And many clones are more than Jovian—the long lines of Evanders and the Andrews have multiplied with humans at a rapid rate. The propensity for violence lies within them and the hybrids they've sired. What if the humans attack them, and they retaliate instead of disarm?"

Jimmy shook his head, dismissing the possibility. "Look, Evander," he said in a fatherly way, "you've already created the laws and legislation needed to protect both clones and humans. The rest was always going to be out of your hands."

In other words, Evander thought, *it is written in the stars*, an answer Uncle Jimmy had often given his mother.

It seemed he would make no further headway with Uncle Jimmy than he'd made with Caroline. "If you're not here to help with the humans," Evander said, "why are you here?"

"I've come to see the kids," Jimmy said, with a look that let Evander know he should already be aware of this.

"You mean, mine? Dmitri and Natasha."

"Yes, your children."

Having been away from Earth for so long, Jimmy had never met the children—or even his wife, Nadia, come to think of it. A sudden urgent need to see them didn't make sense. "Why now?" Evander asked.

"I want to examine them. It's important we get to the bottom of this."

Jimmy knew about Natasha. Or . . . did he?

"And by 'this' you mean . . . " Evander waited.

"The boy's muscular indisposition."

Doctors didn't know what to call Dmitri's disability. They settled on "a rare disease similar to muscular dystrophy" to describe it. His muscles failed him all the while his brain excelled.

"There's been no change since he was born," Evander said, "but Dmitri's doing well. He's in school. Sharp as a whip. They call him 'the locksmith' because his main interest lies in the cluster of keys he plays with."

"And the girl," Jimmy said in a telling way, "are you certain she has inherited your father's affliction?"

Evander and Nadia had spoken to no one outside of the cardiologist about Natasha's trouble, which meant the oneness still worked, at least for Uncle Jimmy. Evander wondered whether he should be relieved about that, or worried.

"Two days ago, Natasha injured a rib playing on school grounds. Her doctor called for a set of X-rays, and one of them raised a red flag. She didn't like what she saw, so she did some tests."

"A human doctor?"

Jovians in general didn't respect the human medical profession. "Yes, a human doctor."

"Have you discussed it with David? He may have a simple answer."

"There was no answer at all when my father was diagnosed."

"That's correct, but like humans, Jovians have learned quite a bit in twenty-five years. It's possible a transplant, or something else, could be an easy answer."

An easy answer. One of the Jovian elite could never understand how hard it would be to convince a child's human mother that removing her daughter's heart and replacing it with a foreign object might be the answer—let alone an easy one. Especially when that child appeared to be as healthy as a morning in May. "A decision of this magnitude is in no way easy, James."

"Of course, of course." Uncle Jimmy rubbed his forehead in a stressful manner.

"It hasn't even been confirmed by a second physician yet."

Jimmy took the pinecone from his pants pocket and jiggled it like change in the palm of his hand. "I think you know it's a matter better handled by Jovians. And I'm only saying it may not be as dire as it seems."

That sounded suspicious. "What do you know?"

Jimmy's face fell, void of expression. "I may have glimpsed the future the other day and—"

Evander's breath caught in his throat. He grasped at this bit of hope as if it were a rope thrown into the pit of despair that threatened to consume him. "You saw her? You saw Natasha in the future? Fully grown, an adult?"

"I saw *evidence* of her. I'm sorry to be evasive, but that's all I can say."

Evander sank back into his worry, too afraid to accept this vague observation as good news.

Uncle Jimmy extended an apology by way of the softness in his eyes.

Empathy, Evander thought.

"Look," Uncle Jimmy said, "you can't control the world, and neither can I. None of us can."

Evander's helplessness dropped like a stone into his stomach. "I realize that, believe it or not." He gazed unseeing at a tray of black flowers beside him. "So, you came to see the kids? Is that all?"

Jimmy's shoulders jerked and his brows arched high across his forehead. "You don't know?"

All Evander knew was that whatever was coming next was going to knock him for a loop. "I haven't been receiving all of the messages. I'm not sure why."

"I'm here about the defenses," Jimmy said.

"Whose defenses?"

"Why, Earth's, of course."

6

F ran noticed the grimace on Lisa's face as he entered the house through the side door in the garage. That clenched-jaw frown—part angry, part concerned— showed up a lot lately. As one of the older nurses in her department, Lisa did her best to get herself to the wellness center and do the occasional yoga or meditation to relieve tension, but since Max had moved back home from school she'd been noticeably on edge.

"Hey." Her flat greeting told Fran all he needed to know about her stress level.

"How's he doing?" he asked.

"I still don't understand how it happened. Even if Max gave the guy attitude, he's the boss's son, and you're always talking about Jovians and nonviolence. Is this Leonard guy a Jovian?"

"He's a clone of Leo. An early one. I still can't believe he threw a punch." Fran placed his security belt on the bench near the door. "Then again, you've seen the news. Things are touchy right now. Most members of the security squad are clones. They're not protesting at Starbright yet, and they probably never will, but what's happening in Philly affects them. It has to."

As Lisa led the way out of the little mud room into the kitchen, Fran unbuttoned the top two buttons of his shirt, the Starbright patch opposite the pocket catching his attention as he noticed some of the stitching that held it firm had come undone.

Lisa's hair appeared frazzled, loose pieces spiraling here and there like corkscrews, as if Max's latest drama caused it to go haywire. She'd been wearing sweats since Max moved back in, and often complained about how much stuff—sneakers, jackets, food wrappers, and empty drink bottles—accrued around the house these days. Staying tidy, she had said, didn't seem possible anymore.

"Will Max even be able to go back to work?" she asked.

"Oh, yeah," Fran said, feigning confidence, "don't worry about that. I'm handling it."

"I'm sure you are." She opened the refrigerator and grabbed a bottle of water, which she held out to him. "Was it his fault?"

He took the water and noticed a lack of activity occurring in the kitchen. Nothing on the stove. No heat rising from the oven. No timers set.

"I'm not sure. Could have been. You know how he is, expecting everything to be easy. Being his complaining self. You can't bring that stuff to the office. Leonard's high ranking and damn good at his job. All of my employees are. It doesn't make sense that he would strike another worker."

Lisa sought out the ceiling, the skin around her eyes trembling with fatigue. "God knows I've done my best to prepare Max for adulthood. You have, too. He's just always been so young for his age. Maybe we were wrong to encourage him to work there. Maybe he isn't ready for the responsibility."

"But Max doesn't have much responsibility at work," Fran said with more zeal than he'd meant to. "All he has to do is whatever I tell him to do—and he's older than I was when I joined the FBI."

"Okay. But you were born mature. Max is a whole other can of worms."

Lisa grabbed the back of a kitchen chair and leaned into it.

"Look," Fran told her, "it'll be fine. I spoke with Leonard, and I don't think he's still angry. Maybe he was just having a day."

"I hope so," she said without conviction.

"Where's Max now?" Fran asked.

"In his room. In the robe, unfortunately."

"Oh, crap. Not the robe again." He released a frustrated laugh. "We should have burned it while we had the chance."

"He put it on as soon as he got home. And you know what that means."

Fran rubbed his hand over the scruff on his chin. "I guess he's going back to the dark side."

She sighed, the frustration weighing her down, making her appear somehow shorter.

"Okay, whatever, damn it," Fran said. "I'm sick of walking on eggshells around him. You and I are going out."

Her face brightened with the prospect of not having to come up with dinner.

"Let's get a beer and some chili at Red Star. You want to? Or, that pesto crostini we had last time. Maybe even a shot or two?"

"I was going to heat up the leftover ziti, but going out sounds better." Lisa tugged at her T-shirt. "Just let me change real quick?"

"Of course, take your time."

"Ten minutes," she yelled from the stairs as she climbed toward their bedroom.

Fran took to the hall in the opposite direction. He knocked Max's door and tried to twist the knob but it was locked. "Hey, you in there? Open up."

At home, the kid wore earbuds most of the time, so Fran knocked again, louder. "Max," he said.

"Food?" Max shouted back.

What did he think this was, a restaurant?

"No. Not food. Open the door. I need to talk to you."

"I'm busy," was the answer. "Come back later?"

Fran's impatience surged through his chest to the tips of his now-buzzing ears. "Open this door before I knock the knob off."

The door creaked back a few inches, and Fran nudged it the rest of the way. Max stepped back, standing before Fran in his off-white terrycloth robe tied at his skinny waist. He wasn't wearing pants underneath, and his athletic socks reached most of the way up his spindly shins.

Fran tried not to smile—or laugh—neither of which he accomplished. "Should your mother and I be worried?"

"What do you mean?" Max looked down at himself. "Why?"

"Because the last time you wore the robe, you were, uh—" Best not to mention the word *depressed*. "I just thought we were past this."

"Um," the kid said, his swollen lip and frowny eyes combining for a pathetic demeanor that stirred Fran's concerned place. "I'm fine. Not my fault this country's gone to hell, and clones will soon rule the earth."

"Don't say that," Fran said. "Clones don't want to rule anything. That's a bullshit conspiracy theory, and you know it. I keep telling you, *they're* the ones who are oppressed.

They want to be treated fairly. Not all of them want to be protectors. Can't say I blame 'em."

"That's not what they're saying on the internet."

"Yeah, well, I told you not to believe most of what you see on that stupid, antiquated piece of technology. Does more harm than good. Who still reads the internet, anyway?"

"I told you, a lot of people do. It's not all lies. Evander cleaned it up."

"He cleaned it up as much as possible." Fran corrected him. "It's still about 50 percent lies. You know you should be getting your news from a Neutral Network source."

"Can I close the door now?" Max said.

"Your mother and I are going out."

"Cool. See you later." The door started to close, but Fran pushed it open again.

"One more thing. Tomorrow morning, you and I need to talk about what happened at work."

"Great," the kid said with a false positivity. "Did you fire him yet?"

"No, Max, I already told you, no one's getting fired."

"Well, did you at least tell Caroline what he did?"

"No need. The problem is handled."

"Fine." Max huffed. "Bring me back something to eat."

"You're joking, right?" Fran laughed angrily. "Do you see a servant here? Put some pants on and join the human—"

"Just please bring me something."

The eye roll that came with that request tempted fate.

"If you don't want to come with us," Fran said, doing a very good job of not losing his cool, "you can fix yourself something from the kitchen. Mom said there's leftover ziti."

He pulled the door closed with a thud.

How did my kid end up like this?

7

Evander found Caroline in the laboratory with Miranda, the real Miranda. None of the Jovian elite struggled to distinguish between clones and the real thing—the age difference gave them away, first of all, as clones were always younger. In general, Jovians reached a certain age in human form and stayed there—their bodies simply didn't progress any further. Caroline would always be a beautiful sixty-something, and Miranda would forever enjoy her forties.

This was just another way in which Evander differed as a Jovian hybrid. Not only had he sprinted through his childhood and young adulthood, but he'd also traveled through space and time in such a way that added even more years to his physical appearance (a fact that benefitted him when it came time to embark on his senatorial campaign).

He seemed to be progressing at a normal human rate at this point, but no one knew for sure whether his body would reach a stopping place, like other Jovian elites had, or continue as a regular human would.

The women sat at the first long table in a series of three,

the way they would at a café waiting for the server to deliver tea. Evander neared, and their conversation ended.

"This looks serious," he said, dressing his words in charm.

"Oh, now," Miranda passed him one of her enthusiastic grins, "it's just two of the sharpest minds on the planet having a conversation."

"No one could disagree with that," he said, feigning pleasantness. Meanwhile, Caroline's demeanor matched that of a student in statistics class, albeit the smartest of students, and more than a little bored by the lesson.

He hovered in front of them, waiting for an invitation to have a seat.

Miranda set her eyes on him, her dimples appearing out of nowhere. "You know, Evander, I never told you, but you're even more handsome in person than you are on television. I can honestly say the cameras don't do you justice."

Was this flattery or insult? He sensed a vague aura of jealousy and irritation coming from her, more so than usual.

"What are you ladies up to?" he asked. "Scheming to take over the world—or maybe just the human population?" He chuckled at his attempt at humor but knew too well that Jovians didn't joke.

Miranda cackled, and while it almost sounded real, the problem as Evander saw it was that she didn't feel laughter the way humans did. The result was the laughter of a mediocre actor.

"You've definitely inherited aspects of your mother's personality," she said. "Svetlana possessed some dominant genes, I'll give her that. And, to answer your question, Jovians already rule the human world, whether humans are aware of it or not. I think you know that."

Then she stood, her cheerfulness evaporating as she pushed her chair back and stepped away.

Evander didn't reply, and Miranda didn't seem to expect

him to. She passed Elsa and Martin as she continued on her way into the corridor without another word.

Evander lowered into her chair.

Caroline imparted no warmth, no smile nor gentle rise of her brow. She never played at being human—as far as Evander knew, the idea never crossed her mind. Jovians were not at their best in human form, and yet Caroline's beauty was as disarming as any human's. Her golden brown eyes, fascinating in their own right, somehow reflected both softness and sharpness at the same time. Her classic features came together in a symmetrical whole—a small, straight nose, perfectly oval head, striking (but not heavy-handed) brows, severe cheekbones.

"You've spoken with James," she said, as if the words appeared upon his forehead.

"Yes, and I have to say, I'm disappointed. I didn't save the planet so that humans could go to war. Not with clones and not with some galactic species whose attack may or may not be imminent."

This seemed to interest her. She clasped her hands and rested them on the table. The rare blue diamond on her middle finger glinted. "Why did you save it?"

"Because it was the right thing to do," he said, though a deeper answer lingered just behind this first one, and he did nothing to stop it from emerging. "And because Earth is brimming with life and miraculous creatures, and beauty, intelligence, creativity . . . and love."

He wondered if Caroline had any idea what love was.

Her mouth quirked before she responded, "And violence and hatred, and all of those other human emotions, like greed and sadness and jealousy."

"Mm," he said. "I also love it because Earth is my home, and the home of my wife and children."

She granted him a curt nod. Jovians knew what it meant

to love (and miss) their home planet. Perhaps that was one of the reasons Edmund had left.

"I want to ask you something, but I'm afraid you'll be disappointed by the question," Evander said, slowly. "Please forgive me if I'm out of line, but . . . you don't like humans, do you?" Not so long ago he and Caroline delved candidly into many difficult topics, and he wished they could go back to that kind of relationship. "It's funny," he continued, "until recently I'd never considered whether you liked them or didn't like them. I suppose I assumed you cared for them the way a parent unconditionally cares for a child."

She had waited, unmoving, for him to finish.

"It's not a matter of fondness, I assure you," she said. "I told you the human race is in the throes of an evolutionary leap, a natural and unstoppable occurrence. Granted, this leap is happening much faster than human evolution has in the past, but I suggest you don't concern yourself about it."

"Tell me the truth, and please don't be offended." He spoke in a hushed tone, leaning in with kindness. "Do you know what love is? Have you ever felt it?"

She turned away, her hair sweeping her face. "That is not the issue, I'm afraid."

He closed his mouth and pushed back into the chair. "Okay, well, I'm sorry, but I need an answer. What are we doing? We evolved the race, instilled the Jovian way of nonviolence, cleaned the air, cooled the planet. We basically prevented an apocalypse. You always said there was a bigger reason for all of this, that the universe needs Earth. *Jovians* need Earth. What is it needed for?"

"Earth is far more plentiful than any other planet, and the Jovian connection to it goes back millennia," she said in a manner that resembled facts recited from a notecard. "The humans may not realize our connection, but that connection has existed and will continue to exist."

"Are you saying humans think Earth is theirs, but all along it's been the Jovians'?"

"I'm saying it makes no difference what they think. We're here. We've been here for a long time, helping them progress, getting them ready."

"Getting them ready for what?"

Her hesitation spanned a fraction of a second, but he noticed it. It meant something.

"For whatever comes," she said in a serene voice that opposed the gravity of the sentiment.

Evander gazed out the window, observing the trees in the distance. "Uncle Jimmy says we have to prepare our defenses, but he doesn't know what we'll be defending against. I need to know."

"There's nothing for you to do. And James isn't supposed to be here. If it weren't for your daughter, he wouldn't be."

The way she blamed Natasha for James's visit was a step too far, even for her.

"Your great-grandchild has a heart defect," he informed her, as if she didn't already know. "He's here to see if there's anything he can do to help."

"There isn't," she said in her usual, emotionless tone, though this time, her carelessness electrified Evander's nerves. "He probably didn't want to tell you. He's very human in that way; he lies in order to protect feelings."

At that, Evander slipped mentally from the rocky ledge of a cliff and clung by his fingertips in an attempt to avoid the sea of rage that lingered below. He needed to stay clear of rage if he wanted answers. Natasha may die long before her time, and Caroline didn't care. Just like his father had died before his time, and Caroline didn't care. She hadn't shed a tear at Andrew's funeral—Svetlana had made that clear. No wonder Svetlana had hated Caroline with such passion.

Except that Uncle Jimmy said David might be able to help

Natasha, Evander reminded himself, with a swell of hope. *Uncle Jimmy saw evidence of her future.*

"Sometimes I wonder," he said with quiet hesitancy, "if you hate the human side of me as well."

He hadn't meant to go this far and at first regretted saying it. But Caroline remained unaffected, upright in her chair like the queen waiting for a server to pour more tea.

"Jovians don't hate," she said. "I certainly don't hate any part of you. It's the human side that put you in power and allowed you to become the most beloved president in the history of the most powerful nation on this bright blue planet."

That was her pet name for Earth, "the bright blue planet," something she came up with soon after Evander's efforts to heal it had begun to work.

She held her head high, the edges of her bobbed hair razor sharp. She was a royal who owed no one an explanation, the matriarch of a family who merely gave orders to be abided by. "As I said," she told him, "you have played your role well, and there's nothing more for you to do here."

She didn't hate any part of him, but she still wanted him to leave.

8

F ran decided he and Max would work the same shifts. If Fran needed to stay late, Lisa would pick Max up. Max would learn that having a job was more than just doing the job. It was about responsibility and showing up even when you didn't feel like it. Even when you disliked a co-worker. It was about getting along with people and taking orders from those who ranked higher than you.

At 10 a.m., Fran left Leonard in charge of the crew and drove with Max into town. He needed to stop at the hardware store and pick up some basic supplies. Miscellaneous this and that in an effort to rid Starbright International of whatever cryptic buzz bothered Queen Jovian. The hardware store occupied a building across the street from the town cemetery. As they drove past the entry to the graveyard, he spotted something bright orange in the middle of it. It was puffy like a parachute.

Max derailed his train of thought when he said, "Is that a tent?"

Some nutjob is camping in the cemetery?

How had the cops not noticed? Granted, ever since the

UFO sighting that occurred in 1965, Kirksberg had been famous for strange occurrences, and strange human beings had been both visiting and making Kirksberg their home since that time. *But still.* Who the hell chose to camp in a graveyard?

Fran pulled into the nearest parking space and undid his seat belt, then told Max to "Stay put."

"What? No," Max said.

Fran stepped out of the car. When he reached the sidewalk, he heard the passenger-side door open behind him.

"I told you to stay put," he said over his shoulder. "I expect you to do as I say. Get back in the car, Max. I mean it."

Max stood on the grass that lined the walk. He didn't get back in the car, but he didn't follow either.

Fran had crossed under the cemetery's wrought-iron threshold when footsteps came up behind him. *He literally cannot stay in the car*, he thought. *Unbelievable.*

"Fine," Fran said, vaguely shaking his head. "Come on then."

Together they reached the bright orange tent and peered inside at a crumpled sleeping bag, flashlight, and an open book with a pencil resting in its gutter. Fran crouched his way in and lifted the book, a dusty hardcover of the sort you'd find in the reference or archives section of the library. It opened to an illustration of the human heart. *A medical text? How many doctors camp in the cemetery? This is beyond bizarre,* Fran thought.

He stared into the distance and realized his gaze led to where his friends' headstones stood. As far as he could see, there were no signs of vandalism or foul play, but maybe he should visit the Jovian plot to make sure. "I'll be right back," he told Max and headed in that direction.

"Where are you going?" Max followed like a scent hound.

"I just need to . . . " Fran's words trailed off. He felt no obligation to explain.

It had been some time since he'd visited his friends' graves, and he didn't know why, but now that he'd reached them, the sadness he normally kept locked tight clawed its way through metal bars he hadn't noticed were loose. His mourning and loss resurfaced with such unexpected brawn that he had to turn away so Max wouldn't see the heat of emotion that warmed his nose and clouded his vision.

And then he made an inadvertent sniffling sound.

"Are you crying?" Max did nothing to stifle his surprise— or the volume of his voice—and Fran cringed, not that anyone was nearby to hear.

He rubbed his nose and cleared his throat. "Course not," he said in the deepest octave he could reach.

Max seemed both drawn and perplexed, a squint pinching his face. "Don't get mad, okay," he said after a moment, "but was, like, Svetlana a girlfriend when you and Mom split up for those couple of years?"

Fran hated thinking about the years he and Lisa went their separate ways. After the day in the park, when David transformed into his true alien form, Fran began to research the Jovian family as a whole. For a time, he became obsessed with them; he even searched their homes and recorded the comings and goings of employees at Starbright. To this day, Lisa didn't believe the Jovians were anything but wealthy eccentrics in spite of what Fran claimed to have happened. She accepted that they were strange and that strange things happened around them, but not Fran's explanation of aliens from Jupiter. And Fran had always respected the line she'd drawn, figuring her brain just wouldn't let her go there.

"No, Max, she wasn't a girlfriend. Not at all. She was married to my best friend. And I cared for her a lot—for *both* of them. Mom and I split for other reasons. We didn't agree on some important stuff. That's all. And then I lost my arm," he added.

"Oh, yeah. Sometimes I forget," Max said.

Fran gazed at his friends' headstones. "You know, Andrew died without warning. And I'm still pissed about it. You've had a best friend before, so just think about what that would be like."

The kid shut his mouth and sought out the ground.

"Then Svetlana was here one second and gone the next." Fran blew out an exhale and shook his head, still feeling how unfathomable it was that he'd never see her again.

With slow caution, Max reached up and placed a hand on Fran's back, but then he pulled it away a second later.

"Anyway," Fran said, hoping to end the conversation on that note.

Unfortunately Max had never been very good at reading social cues.

"You said Andrew was a Jovian, but he was different than his parents. He wasn't a wealthy weirdo like the rest of his family, right?"

Fran inhaled as he reminded himself of the importance of patience. "*Weirdo* is kinda harsh, but the Jovians are eccentric, that's true," he said, knowing full well *eccentric* didn't cover the half of it, but that was as much as Max needed to know. "And no, Andrew wasn't like them. Not at all. He was normal. When it came to his family, he played to the beat of his own drum."

"Uh-huh," Max said with hesitation. "I don't know what you mean by that."

"It means he did things his own way. He didn't follow his relatives' lead." Fran cleared his throat with a gruff cough. The less Max knew about the Jovians, the better.

The spring breeze rushed through newly sprouted leaves

above their heads, like chattering children without a care in the world.

"What happened to Svetlana?" Max asked. "You told me she didn't die, but I haven't seen her, and, well, there's a headstone with her name on it right there."

"Yeah, I know it's strange. She's gone. I guess that's all that matters."

Now was not the time to tell Max that Svetlana had traveled to a different universe, if that was even what she'd done. Fran wished one of the Jovians would confirm what had happened to her, to assure him it all worked out, that she'd reached wherever it was she'd wanted to go, but when he'd asked (and he hadn't asked in a long time), a concrete answer never came.

"Why can't you just tell me?" Max said. "I mean, there has to be a reason."

Fran didn't appreciate his pushiness. He didn't want Max to know that Svetlana had climbed into a spaceship and rocketed out of this universe or galaxy, or whatever it was she'd done. He didn't want to put "leaving the planet" out there period. He already knew Max dreamed of better places that may or may not exist.

But then Max said, "Leonard told me about humans who visit different places in space. Not astronauts, but something else. . . . *Travelers*, I think he called them. He said there's a program at Starbright. Maybe Svetlana became a traveler?"

An angry thrum of protectiveness drummed the walls of Fran's mind. He never should have let the kid step into Starbright. What the hell was he thinking, encouraging Max to take this job, even if it was only temporary. They were surrounded by Jovians. Of course he would hear things. Of course he would ask questions.

"Leonard had no business telling you that. It's a company

secret. One of many. Don't ever tell anyone what you just told me, do you understand?"

"So it's true?" Max said, unable to hide his delight. "Svetlana left Earth. She went into outer space?"

Fran couldn't lie or refuse to answer the question. If he did, Max might make it a research project. He might attempt to interview Leo or, God forbid, Caroline.

"Uh, yeah, that's right. She traveled. But not like the other travelers. She was Andrew's wife, so they did something special for her."

"Like what? Gave her a first-class ticket?" Max chuckled.

"Not exactly. More like they gave her a *one*-way ticket, and she's never coming back. I'll never see her again. Worse, I don't know whether she got where she hoped to go."

Max's good cheer dried up and fell away. "Why don't you just ask them?"

That was a legitimate question.

"I did ask them once, and I didn't get an answer. Besides, it's not my place to ask. I'm not part of the family. I'm just an employee. And that's how it is. They have their secrets, and I respect that. You should, too."

"But you really want to know, and you could just ask. I don't see why—"

Fran groaned a little, wishing to God he'd been born with more patience. "Let's drop it, okay? I didn't mean to go down memory lane this morning, you know?"

"That's fair," Max said. "Sorry to make you relive the whole thing. I'm sure Svetlana ended up in a better place."

"That *was* the plan, but that's also what they say when people die, so . . . " He shrugged as the sadness crept back in.

"Maybe it's true about going to a better place," Max said, apparently *not* able to drop it. "I mean, I hope I get to a better place at some point. A better place sounds good to me."

At that, Fran's ears burned—Max seemed unaware that

his bouts of depression had led to seriously worrisome thoughts on the part of his parents. "Please don't ever let your mother hear you say that."

"I'm just saying, the world we live in is pretty much shit."

His carefree tone made Fran want to shake some sense into him, to tell him, "This is the life you've been given. Please make the most of it."

Instead, he said, "After all Evander did to clear the air and reverse the global warming, and basically save the whole damn planet? You should be optimistic. The future looks pretty bright for your generation. A lot brighter than it did for mine."

Max glared at Fran as if *he* were the naïve one taking part in this conversation. Then he said, "Evander didn't exactly smooth the tension between humans and clones and the pathetic way human beings think they're the only species that matters." He paused there to seethe, a hint of pink spreading like watercolor over his tawny cheeks. "I mean, I'm not saying it's so bad I'd rather be dead."

"Well, I'm happy to hear that," Fran said, genuinely glad the kid had said it out loud without having to be asked.

"But the world's far from perfect and," Max added, "I think you know Earth isn't exactly my happy place."

The thought of Max leaving the planet softened Fran's defenses. "I know it isn't. But you have to understand, the world will never be anything close to perfect. Besides, perfection is overrated."

"Well, things could be better. A lot better."

"Maybe," Fran said with a shrug. "Or maybe not."

He couldn't change Max's opinions when it came to the world at large. An easy "You don't understand" or "It'll get better" or "It's not so bad" would never do the trick. The kid's streak of negativity ran a chasm straight to his giving-up place. Healing that chasm, filling that void with "better" things, Fran expected, would take a lifetime.

He gazed at his friends' headstones and remembered how shortly before Svetlana took off in that pod, she'd made him call Lisa. Made him take the first step to getting his life back with her and Max. If Svetlana hadn't pressed him, he might never have done it. Fran could have spent the rest of his days sad and alone, drunk at Holy Shot's, and Max could have lived his whole life hating him.

Fran never had the chance to thank Svetlana for getting him back on track, back to his family. Sometimes the urge to call her came over him, and he'd reach for his phone before he remembered calling wasn't an option—there was no way to reach her.

"Look, we better hurry up and get to the hardware store. There's work to do." Sometimes putting your head down and going back to work was the only way to stay sane.

They started down the path toward the orange tent.

"I like that idea, though," Max said, breaking the silence. "Traveling? I might want to do that one day for real."

Fran whipped his head in Max's direction with every intention of listing the many reasons he'd never let that happen, but then he saw the light in the kid's eyes. Rays of optimism. The hope that had been lost for years beaming through Max's chasm of negativity. And Fran couldn't do it; he couldn't snuff out the dream.

"You think they need a master of avionics on one of those flights?" Max's cheeks bulged with optimism. "They probably need a whole team of 'em, right?"

Thank God they don't let just anyone do it, Fran thought.

He shut down his urge to dissuade. "Not sure," he muttered, more determined than ever to keep a close eye on his son.

9

The next morning, as Evander stepped out the front door of his residence, sunlight spread yellow rays across the lawn. To his left and his right, stood Elsa and Martin, ready to start the workday.

"Have I mentioned I don't need you two anymore?"

"Martin apprehended an interloper last night," Elsa said in her usual even timbre. "Which is only one of the reasons I refuse to hear your request to decline protection."

Evander glanced at tall, slender Martin, whose ears stuck out from his nearly shaved head. As usual, Martin stood unassuming, quiet, on alert. "An interloper? Well, thank you, Martin. Impressive work, as always." Evander wasn't convinced that the interlopers Elsa mentioned on occasion actually existed. If they'd been real, he would've sensed danger. Not all of his telepathic senses were down.

"I'm well trained to do my job, sir."

Martin sometimes sounded like a robot, as did Elsa. And that made sense because their AI faculties not only made them stellar at their jobs but also affected their thought patterns.

The van waited in the drive. Elsa opened the door and peered inside, then gestured Evander in before she and Martin joined. The driver's compartment remained empty. Elsa or Martin used some kind of cognitive power to communicate with the van. Outside of being told when to turn on and off and where to go, the van drove itself. Quite well, at that. They'd never been involved in an accident.

At Starbright, Evander entered through the front of the building. Before the sun rose that morning, Caroline had texted to say he could find David in the astronomical observatory. Usually if David wanted him to know something, he'd impart it through the oneness. It pained Evander to think the strongest of Jovians had to rely on antiquated methods of discourse to get a message to him. But that's what it had come to.

He took the corridor that led to the observatory, then stared into the iris scanner and the doors disappeared into the floor. Former FBI agent and his parents' old friend, Fran Vasquez, had security down to a science, probably as tight as the Pentagon, not that he needed to. Jovians always knew when someone was coming for them. At least, when the oneness was working. But maybe it was working for the others. Maybe Caroline wanted him out of the way more than she let on, and for this reason, she'd cut him off from the rest of the family.

Would she? he wondered.

Then again, Caroline hadn't known Jimmy was back. Evander remembered her flash of surprise when he'd mentioned Jimmy's name and asked if he was there at her request. That meant she was having some trouble with the oneness as well. He had to believe it wasn't his problem alone.

He moved through the corridor at a quick pace, Elsa and her asymmetric white hair and pantsuit two steps ahead, and

Martin with his dark buzz cut and smart suit, two behind. When they reached the door at the end of the hall, he hovered in front of yet another square screen and then waited for Elsa and Martin to do their thing. He was glad for a reason to visit this place; it had been some time since he'd sat in the dark quiet and visually propelled into outer space.

The first time he saw the domed astronomical observatory, with its curved stone walls and oculus on top, he'd felt in his bones a direct line to the universe. Cavernous and cool, the observatory originated in an ancient Peruvian village at least two thousand years ago. Caroline had it excavated and reassembled into the Kirksberg office, claiming Jovian ancestors had built it and therefore it was part of their heritage. Leo said the project had required the help of some president or another, but that was all Evander knew.

Regardless, the observatory became Evander's favorite place to connect with the stars, his absent father (whose spirit resided within a star, in this universe, anyway), and his Jovian roots. It was a place where he could ease into the ancient combination of earthy darkness and vast galaxy, and just be.

While Elsa and Martin carried out a perfunctory check of the observatory's shadowy interior, Evander took in the sparkling veil of dust that hovered like a cloud near its top, the liquid morning sunshine flowing golden through the oculus. The air clung damp to his skin, a scent akin to river mist coming from the stone walls. As his sight adjusted, Evander recognized more fully the details of the telescope situated below—like a boulder stationed in the center of the room, the Starbright prototype incorporated two high-performance mirrors and a meniscus lens powerful enough to produce views of the Jovians' home planet. Beyond its metal bulk, the green glow of a computer screen revealed a cluster of small tables and chairs pushed to the right-hand side. Just a few feet away from that, balanced on a stool in perhaps the darkest area, David sat.

Evander had sensed him before he saw him, and that gave him some solace—evidence that at least some of his Jovian intuition still worked.

David occupied the lithe body of a twentysomething; a near-twin of Evander's father, Andrew, though Evander doubted he ever would have mistaken them. David sat with his feet flat on the floor. His hands rested on his thighs. He said nothing by way of greeting and appeared to be meditating. As Evander neared, he noticed David's eyes moving like the needle of a seismograph beneath his closed lids.

"David?" Evander whispered, stopping a few feet in front of him.

His lids popped open, and Evander reacted by steeling himself. The strength of David's eyes never failed to startle him. In color, they echoed his father's and his own, but not in likeness. Andrew had kind, expressive eyes, from what he'd seen in photographs, while David's proved sharp and cerebral, Jovian through and through. "The opposite of human," he remembered his mother saying.

At the sight of Evander, David did not flinch or gasp. He made no expression at all.

"Good to see you," Evander said, stepping backward to grab one of the nearby chairs. "Is this all right? Caroline told me I could meet you here."

David clasped his hands and rested them on his lap. "I've been waiting." An eerie, not-quite-conscious aura clouded his features, as if he were physically present but mentally overwhelmed by whatever was going on inside of his head. Evander recognized the state, having been there before. David no doubt took it to the nth degree, however. Like Uncle Jimmy, he'd always seemed a lot more brain than body.

"Communications are difficult to decipher these days,"

Evander said, once again trying to conceal the degree to which the oneness was failing him.

He felt some relief when David responded with, "Yes."

"What's the problem, do you know?"

"There has been some type of interference, cosmic or otherwise."

"Caused by?"

"I haven't yet made that determination."

David remained unmoving. He appeared to be conserving all bodily energy for his mind's use. "There are other challenges having to do with the growth of the family as well," he added.

"You mean the clones?" Evander asked.

"The clones. Correct."

That made sense. David was the center of the Jovian oneness. Every Jovian thought passed through him into the oneness, even the thoughts of hybrids and their offspring. Every individual with Jovian blood running through their veins could hear Caroline clearly, but not every one of them could hear, say, Leonard of the security squad. A hierarchy existed in which some voices emerged like puffs of white noise while others spun up like tornadoes, impossible to ignore.

No matter what Jovian clones and descendants did and where they did it, they shared in the oneness.

"So, now you have too much to listen to?" Evander asked.

David answered, without a hint of emotion: "Five hundred eighty-nine thousand four hundred fifty-six new voices. And counting."

"Nearly six hundred thousand," Evander said. "Basically an army."

David gave no reply.

"Did Caroline tell you that I'm disturbed by what's happening in Philadelphia?"

David's lips twitched as if this news amused him. "She didn't have to. I can still hear you."

"Of course you can" Evander said. "The problem is, I'm not hearing you very well. Or anyone else."

"The lack of communication is not intentional. Whatever is happening is out of my hands."

This was a strange admittance for David to make. He was the closest thing to perfection that Evander had ever known.

And yet Caroline had allowed Evander to assume the problem was his alone. Why was she withholding?

More and more it was becoming clear that not only did Caroline want him out of the inner circle, she had already pushed him out, and he hadn't realized it.

"It isn't intentional," David said, responding to that thought.

Evander bowed his head. "It sure seems that way."

"Things are not always as they seem."

After that, David's expression changed. He was like a person whose consciousness occasionally submerged into a vat of thick, sound-absorbing mud. He resumed REM activity, orbs bobbing and twitching under the lids.

Evander took a moment to wonder why Caroline was playing games. Why not tell him what was happening?

Suddenly David's lids popped open. "It's evolution. You can't stop it."

He'd spoken as if joining the middle of someone else's conversation.

"You mean, the problems between humans and clones?" Evander asked.

"Yes. But that doesn't mean you can't make it better for them. Your worry is warranted. And I understand. They're the weaker race." David spoke with bluntness, and he stared dull and unseeing into the distance. Evander wondered if he was saying what Caroline wanted him to say. Perhaps she'd been listening to their conversation from the very beginning and spoke to David internally now.

David continued, "Still, there's no point in trying to stop evolution. The world is ever-changing, ever expanding. Time moves forward naturally, even when one goes back. Your mother, for instance." He blinked suddenly, as if waking from sleep, then turned his head until he came upon Evander.

"How is my mother?" Evander asked.

"I have no connection to Svetlana. You know that."

"I just wondered if you knew anything. Anything at all. For instance, did she make it back to my father? I realize there's no way she *didn't* make it back. But I can't help but wonder whether it worked out for her."

"I'm not all knowing," David said. "She's in a different universe in which Jovians don't exist."

It was the same answer David had provided years ago, the last time Evander inquired.

Evander pressed his lips together and nodded. "I know. I'm sorry. There's a lot going on." He thought of little Natasha and her heart, and the threat that may or may not attack Earth, and how the lack of oneness left him off-balance. For the first time in his life, he felt unsure—and admitting that frightened him.

"I haven't yet deciphered the entity that's planning to attack," David said.

Funny how that worked: when Evander wanted to, he kept his thoughts from most others: Miranda and Leo, occasionally Caroline. But never David. To David, he was more than an open book; he was an open window.

"But you know it's out there?"

"There's a chance, mathematically, that points to it. I believe it will happen."

"Caroline seems to think I can't help with this," Evander said.

"You can help by going to Io."

"You think I should go?"

"I do."

Evander couldn't fathom how that would help. He felt more and more the way his mother must have felt in her attempts to puzzle through a Jovian conundrum.

"And what about my family, my children? They're human. They can't go to Io. They're too young, undeveloped. They won't survive."

"That's what I admired about your mother," David said, invading Evander's space with his penetrating gaze. "As attached as she was to you, she knew what she had to do. She made the right choice, as hard as that was for her."

"I helped her make that choice, David," Evander said, unable to stop the anger from affecting his voice. "*I* was the one who convinced her to go."

"And now you must choose the same for yourself."

A spike of shivers climbed his spine and spread over his scalp. "How can you say that when you know about Natasha's heart? *You know* I can't leave right now. I have many legitimate reasons not to do what Caroline wants me to do."

David's expression didn't change, nor did his body move. His words came from his mouth and yet Evander felt them enter his brain even before he spoke them. "Nevertheless, this is what you must do."

10

That afternoon, Fran took Max outside to teach him how to patrol the Starbright grounds.

"Outdoor teams normally make the rounds twice a day," he said, "changing the times each day so it's unpredictable. Can't let anyone who might be staking out the building figure out when we'll show up. We have to stay on our toes, for obvious reasons."

"Right," Max said, a dull disinterest clouding his demeanor.

"Are you even listening?"

"What? Yes. Patrol twice a day. Different times. Stay on toes. Got it."

Fran nodded, impressed. "Okay, so what equipment will you carry on your person?"

"Pepper spray, taser, cuffs. Uh, I think that's all?"

"And when do you use these things?"

"To apprehend. Or in self-defense."

"Good."

The kid walked at a snail's pace. Fran waved him on. "Pick it up a bit. This isn't supposed to be a leisurely stroll."

Max gave him a numb-faced look before saying, "I really want to work with spacecraft. You know, navigation tools, radar systems, general electronics. Doesn't Caroline know anyone at NASA?"

Fran gazed into the surrounding forest and released a chuckle of sarcasm. "I'm sure she does, and what does that have to do with you?"

"Maybe she could help me get a job doing what I'm trained to do. I mean, my degree is in avionics technology. I'm not cut out for security. This is *your* thing."

"Right. But you can't find a job doing your thing right now, which is why you're doing my thing. You said you were grateful for the job."

"Uh-huh," Max said, and then he caught sight of Fran's extended glare and jumped to say, "I mean, yes, sir, I am. I'm grateful, sir."

"Okay," Fran said with a laugh. "And what are you thinking, anyway? You think you're just going to walk into NASA, and they'll roll out the carpet and ask you what position you want? You have to work your way up. That's what I did. That's what everybody has to do."

Max didn't know. Why would he? Before this, he'd never had a job outside of busboy or convenience store cashier.

Fran considered his own early years of employment and whether he'd ever, in his entire life, been *that* naïve. He had to have been, right? No one popped out of the womb knowing how to be a good employee. But FBI work had come easy to him. A natural fit. Like he was born to do it. His parents must have subliminally prepared him. His dad had been a decorated agent, after all.

They walked along the fence line, Fran scanning for anything unusual, anything that might indicate someone had breached the perimeter the way he and Svetlana once did in search of Jovian secrets. He smiled to himself, realizing that indeed he had been naïve—both he and Svetlana had been—about the Jovians back then. Then again, not many people to this day knew who the Jovians were, outside of being a wealthy and powerful family with interests that lie in the cosmos.

The general public had no idea how far the Jovian reach went.

Leo appeared in the distance, wearing his usual dress pants and button shirt, his hand in his pocket, jangling change. He stood at the base of the cement staircase that led to the back entrance, tipping his head toward the sky and letting the sun hit his face while he waited for someone.

Me maybe? Something must be up.

Fran waved. "Hey, Leo," he said loud enough to reach him.

"Follow me," he told Max, and they broke into a jog.

"Good to see you, Mr. Vasquez." Leo turned in Max's direction. "I see you're showing Max here the ropes."

"Yes, sir," Max said, just like Fran had taught him to.

It wasn't like he was incapable of learning.

"He's a good teacher," Max said.

Leo's focus lingered for another second on Max before returning to Fran. "I'd like to speak to you in private, if you don't mind. You have a few minutes?"

"Of course." Fran ordered Max to "finish patrolling the perimeter. Then come inside and get to work on that issue with the comms system. I'll meet you there."

"Will do." The kid made a curt salute so humorous in its seriousness that Fran had to hold off a laugh as he followed Leo into the building. They passed through the mysterious, completely empty, red-lighted room that led into the lobby. Then they took the spiral staircase to the balcony, which brought them to the Jovian family wing.

Leo was a nice guy, but Fran didn't consider him a friend. He didn't even talk to him on any kind of regular basis, though weekly or at least monthly meetings would have been the norm at any other company. Come to think of it, he'd only been to Leo's office a handful of times. The room contained nothing memorable, empty except for a desk and two chairs: one behind the desk, the other in front of it. No bookshelves or framed certificates or family photos. No lamp, computer, pencil-and-pen cup. Just the desk and two chairs, and a ceiling light.

The kind of weird Fran had come to expect from Jovians.

Leo sat in the large leather chair and rolled up to the desk, then gestured for Fran to sit in the much smaller, less comfortable wooden chair in front. "It has come to my attention that Leonard struck your son," he said.

Fran should have known it was coming, but he'd mostly forgotten about it, and for that reason the statement crashed over him like an Arctic wave. Someone on the team must have talked. He hoped this didn't mean he'd have to fire Leonard.

"It's not a problem, sir," Fran said, uncomfortable in the wood chair, whose back seemed unforgivingly perpendicular. "We've resolved the issue. It won't happen again. Leonard just had a bad—"

"That's what I figured." Leo made a steeple of his fingers. "Look, the security squad prides itself on the stellar work they do. And you've done a first-rate job as their leader." He rolled back a foot or two. The chair made of plush leather resembled in some ways a large hand with Leo cradled in its palm.

"Thank you, sir."

Then Leo tilted his head and shrugged a little. "The problem is, Starbright doesn't permit violence of any sort. We have a zero-tolerance policy, as you well know."

"Yes, sir," Fran said with enthusiasm. "And there haven't been any instances until—"

"Which is one too many." Leo passed him a knowing glance.

Fran sank deeper into the chair, his body like putty oozing down a board meant to support it. "Yes, sir."

"And your son was involved."

A fist-full of heat forced its way into Fran's face. Never in all his years of work—here or at the FBI—had anyone made him blush. But this was about Max. His son. *His* responsibility. The child he'd raised for most of his life. He often wondered whether many of Max's problems originated during those years Fran and Lisa had gone their separate ways.

Just thinking about that dark time brought back a familiar feeling of sick.

"I'm not going to discuss this with Caroline," Leo went on. "I honestly feel there's no need. It's likely she already knows, of course," he said, pausing for effect, "and I wanted to warn you that she may do something about it."

Fran rested his gaze on the wall just beyond Leo, avoiding eye contact in this way. How humiliating. *Damn kid!* Leonard would probably be fired over this. And the rest of the squad would hold it against Max—and himself. This was not going to be good for morale, to say the least. Especially with all that was happening in Philadelphia.

"I understand," Fran said, the cracks of embarrassment showing in his withered reply.

"So, suffice it to say, this is me giving you a heads-up," Leo said. "Other than that, all is well, and please keep doing the A-plus job you've always done." He rolled up to his desk and took a more formal, upright position, ready to get back to the work of the day, though there was not a file, paper, or digital screen of any kind in the immediate area.

"Thank you, sir," Fran said with all the false pleasantness

he could muster. He jumped to his feet and stifled an urge to bow.

What is it about these people that makes me feel so inferior?

"You are very welcome," Leo said.

Fran backed out of the office for some reason instead of turning around.

"Oh, and Fran?" Leo said, examining his fingernails. "Don't let it happen again."

"No, sir," he said loud and clear, much the same way he would have replied to the director of the FBI.

11

That afternoon, Evander took the self-driven van home with Elsa and Martin.

As they pulled into the drive, the team of agents who guarded Nadia and the kids reported all clear. The van's sliding door whooshed open, and Elsa exited first. Evander followed with Martin at his heels. They walked in a line to the front door, Elsa opened it to let Evander in, and then she closed it behind him. After that, Elsa and Martin would take their usual posts at the front and back entries of the house.

Alone at last, Evander hung his suit jacket on a hanger in the foyer's coat closet, then walked through the kitchen, warm with traces of a home-cooked meal. He greeted whatever staff happened to be there, always making a point to say hello to those who served him at work or at home. He arrived in the garden room, still bright with late afternoon light.

Nadia was seated on the couch, and Dmitri sprawled over the coffee table in front of it, his long, thin body clothed in navy-blue flannels, a light wool blanket wrapped around his lower half, which was anchored on the floor. He was so small and thin: it was hard to believe he'd celebrated his eighth birthday not long ago.

Evander smiled at Nadia and waved at Dmitri, then jerked a little when he heard a familiar voice say, "How'd you like that one?"

On the carpet in the area the kids kept their many toys and various entertainment, Uncle Jimmy stood in front of Natasha and rolled a rubber ball off his head. It landed at his feet. He lifted it, then grabbed two more balls he found in a basket behind him, and began to juggle.

"Uncle Jimmy!" Natasha squealed with delight. "How do you do that?"

"Didn't your parents tell you? I'm *magic*," he said, shifting his eyes side to side in a clownish manner.

"Daddy you're home! You didn't tell me Uncle Jimmy was magic," she said, full of fascination and zeal, the kind of boundless joy young children possess.

Evander held up his hands. "I wasn't absolutely sure, so I kept it to myself."

Uncle Jimmy tossed the balls in a fluid manner that even Evander found impressive. He hadn't expected to meet Jimmy at home but welcomed his presence. He wanted him to make good on his promise to examine the children, and, more than that, it was nice to have someone from the family over—someone who wouldn't scowl at their centuries-old, three-story Colonial the way Caroline had when she first saw the house.

She was all about the glamour. Nothing less than a mansion or chateau would do. Strange, considering the gas planet she came from.

Both he and Nadia loved the house as soon as they stepped inside, but it was the garden room in back that had clinched it for them. With wall-to-wall screened windows that opened into the manicured backyard, it felt more like a porch than a room, and Nadia envisioned spending much time there. She dubbed it the "garden room," saying it was "like the outdoors without being outdoors," and that was a good thing for the mother of a son who needed help walking and crawling and even sitting up.

The children watched TV programs and played games there, those they'd made up as well as simple classics like Go Fish and Checkers. The room hosted all of their meals and snacks throughout the day. Natasha crayoned her coloring books to the best of her kindergarten ability and dressed her dolls in often questionable outfits while Dmitri either watched his sister or lay nearby and simply listened. Nothing seemed to make him happier than studying the ring of twenty or so antique keys that had fascinated him since he was four years old.

In some ways, they are "normal" children, Evander thought, though the sadness of Natasha's medical problems and Dmitri's lack of physical ability darkened his optimism.

Dmitri's upper body draped across the coffee table's smooth top, one of his hands dangling the keys in front of his eyes. Like a security blanket or teddy bear, the keys went wherever he did, always jangling. On and off throughout the day he stared at them as if they contained some cryptic solution to the world's problems.

Evander used to wish that he'd wake up one morning to the sight of Dmitri running across the backyard the way kids do, kicking a ball or spinning cartwheels across the lawn. After eight years, though, he'd given in to the fact that his son would never do those things. The simple act of sitting up straight challenged Dmitri, and the only one who spun cartwheels was Natasha.

Or, she used to. The cardiologist said that sort of physical exertion might be enough to kill her.

Evander found himself on the couch beside Nadia. He'd

taken a crouch of a pose: hunched over his own legs, elbows to knees, his fist pressed to mouth, teeth digging into his lips. Now that he was home, the worry he carried for his children weighed heavily upon his head, and he experienced a crampy buildup of tension in his neck and jaw. When Dmitri met his gaze, however, he realized how stressed he must look, and winked, putting on a happy face and straightening to a normal position.

Dmitri made no response in return.

Nadia's warm hand on Evander's shoulder reminded him of her presence. He turned to look at her, and she mouthed the words "Are you all right?"

Evander rubbed his forehead. "Just a long day," he said, but the unconvinced way she observed him told him she knew it was more than that. It was only 3 p.m., first of all, and he was already home.

"Lon-ga, lon-ga, lon-ga," Dmitri muttered without taking his focus from the keys or changing his position at all. He often vocalized out of context. Like the muscles in the rest of his body, those that worked his mouth and tongue didn't perform properly, failing to produce the normal speech one expected of an eight-year-old. For this reason, people who didn't know him assumed he lacked smarts, but nothing could have been further from the truth.

Evander reached over and mussed Dmitri's warm hair, an act that caused the child to tense. *Sensitive to touch*, that's what the doctors called it. A condition that stopped Evander and Nadia from hugging him the way they wanted to, the way any parent would want to.

Uncle Jimmy finished his juggling act by letting two balls drop to the carpet and the third to clock him on top of his mostly bald head.

Natasha shouted "Ouch!" then clapped her tiny hands and said, "Again, please!"

"I don't think so," Uncle Jimmy said in the midst of a bow. "If you don't mind, I'm going to sit in that rocking chair beside the couch. Juggling, I'm afraid, is quite taxing on the system. Your father knows that better than anyone in the free world."

Natasha released a fluttering, little-girl giggle. "You mean juggling his schedule, don't you?"

"Exactly, my dear," Uncle Jimmy said, flush with delight. "Boy, you're a smart one."

"You may go." She opened the plastic doctor kit in front of her and proceeded to take out the bright yellow stethoscope. "I have work to do."

"Very resourceful," he said. "*Merci beaucoup.*"

She pointed in the direction of his feet. "Also, your shoe is untied."

Uncle Jimmy glanced downward before falling into the rocking chair and vaulting back and forth at a severe angle. Dmitri raised his head and observed but didn't speak. He was a thinker, not a speaker. Perhaps losing the Jovian oneness hurt Evander the most in the way it kept him from hearing Dmitri and conversing with him telepathically, something they hadn't done for several days now. The kid spoke out loud so infrequently that Evander felt like he was losing him.

"Caroline wants you to go to Io," Jimmy said in a curt, unassuming way that made Evander wonder if he'd heard him correctly.

He didn't appreciate Jimmy bringing it up before he'd had a chance to broach the subject with Nadia. Uncle Jimmy was very good at raising the blood pressure of those around him —Svetlana had mentioned that more than once or twice.

"That was only one of the suggestions Caroline made the last she and I spoke," Evander said.

Jimmy planted his feet on the floor and stopped rocking. "Edmund is there, and there's a problem with the communications. I think he needs help, but something is stopping the messages from getting through."

"David said it's because of the clones. Too many voices. An overload on the system."

Uncle Jimmy shook his head. "I don't think so." Then he twitched and ducked a little in the chair, perhaps spooked by a strange sound.

"What is it?" Evander asked.

"I . . . " Jimmy raised one hand, gesturing for Evander to stop talking, then he tipped back his head and squinted, seemingly listening for something distant and faint.

Dmitri jangled his keys. "I-o, I-o, I-o," he said, sounding like a frog's croak. When Evander glanced at him, Dmitri laughed to himself and said "I-o" again.

Jimmy stood. "I have to be on my way. Don't go, Evander. Thank you for having me in your home. I enjoyed the juggling and . . . " He quickened his pace toward the back door, then opened it and jerked back when he found Martin standing guard there. "Goodbye, Natasha," he said before slamming the door behind him.

Evander shook his head. "Did he just tell me not to go?" He rubbed the five o'clock shadow growing across his chin and wondered if it were possible that running a country was easier than dealing with one's own extended family.

"I am not entirely sure," Nadia said. She made the same long, annoyed face she'd been making lately at any mention of the Jovian family in general. In spite of all she'd been through—leaving her homeland, traveling to Jupiter, becoming the first lady of the country—she was still so Russian. Her accent remained intact as did her way of staying calm through the most unexpected of events. The fates had certainly picked the right woman for him.

Then he recalled why Jimmy had stopped by to begin

with. "He was supposed to examine Natasha. Both children, actually."

"Examine them?" Nadia picked some lint from her pants. "The way a doctor would, you mean?"

"Maybe. I told him what the cardiologist discovered this week," he said under his breath, "and he wanted to look at her."

Nadia paled at the reminder of Natasha's ailing heart. "He spent some time with her before you came home. He spent time with both of the children, sitting with them and talking with them. Dmitri even spoke a few words."

"That's great," Evander said. "Maybe that's all Jimmy needed to do."

Nadia shrugged. "When I first met him at the door, I experienced this indescribable feeling, much worse than what happens with the others." She fluffed her hair with outspread fingers as she spoke. "Those Jovian electrical waves—"

"Buzzing over your scalp," he said, finishing her sentence. "Jimmy is powerful, to say the least. It's probably due to his brain activity, though that's not the scientific explanation." Evander pushed back his sleeves. "And I swear he just told me not to go to Io, which is strange. Then again he's always been strange. Strangest of all Jovians, and you know that's saying a lot."

Nadia threw back her head with a laugh. "It is," she said scrunching her nose in a cute way. Evander loved her face. He'd never tire of it, or her. If only he could assure her that Natasha would be all right.

The doorbell rang three hurried times.

"That's probably him now," Evander said as he rose. "No doubt he's forgotten something, absentminded professor that he is." He passed through the kitchen and traversed the foyer.

Through the glass in the door, he viewed Caroline scrutinizing Elsa, who blocked the way for her and two young Evander clones.

Whenever he encountered clones of himself, Evander wondered if that was what he really looked like as a young man, not that he'd been a young man for long. It was both fascinating and jarring to watch these individuals in action. Like watching an actor impersonate him in a not-quite-right way. He'd been so happy when they'd stopped making the replicas, back when he became a senator. By then, however, they'd already made several thousand (they never told him the exact number) and located them across the country.

He opened the door and put on a pleased expression as Caroline became aware of his presence. His grandmother had been there only once, for the housewarming party Nadia hosted five months prior, yet she barged in now as if she owned the place, the two Evanders following.

"I'm here for Jimmy," she said. "It's urgent."

"I'm afraid you've missed him. He left a half hour ago. Please come in. Nadia and the children will love to see you."

"This isn't a social visit."

Her impending presence must have chased Jimmy away, which made Evander more certain that the "Don't go" was indeed a serious warning. *What the hell was going on?* The obscured communication. Caroline telling him to go to Io. Jimmy telling him not to. It was almost as if the family were breaking in two.

"I've received some information concerning Edmund, and I believe he needs you and Jimmy on Io as soon as possible. The situation is dire. I'd hoped you would make the decision to go on your own, that you'd already be on your way, but now there's no time to waste."

Jimmy had just told him no one had been in touch with Edmund, that the problem with communications had prevented it.

"I might have already left had you expressed some urgency," Evander said coolly. "What's happening on Io?"

"Edmund is dealing with an unintelligent species. He needs your and Jimmy's assistance."

"What kind of unintelligent species? The one preparing to attack Earth?"

"Quite likely," she said, looking down her nose at him. "If you want to save the humans, you'll need to take care of this."

"But Jovians live on Io. Jovians and the Moon Children. Why weren't we informed of this unintelligent species sooner?"

"Communications have been unreliable, as you know."

"Evander," Nadia shouted from the garden room, "you need to see this."

Caroline thrust out her hand to stop him from stepping away. "I'll put an order for your departure in twenty-four hours."

He stared at her slender fingers, thinking her actions strange and desperate.

"The clones are marching up and down the streets of Liberty Square," Nadia shouted. "They're gathering at Independence Lawn in spite of what happened last night. Hurry!"

"Damn it," he said, with an exasperated scowl. "I warned you this would happen. I can't leave now, for many reasons. Natasha—" he started to say, but then stopped himself. She already knew about Natasha and didn't care. "Maybe in a few weeks."

"Your grandfather needs you *now*," Caroline said, squeezing his arm, something she'd never done. "What's happening on Io is far more dire than some skirmish in Philadelphia."

Evander homed in on her tone, her touch, her insistence. Caroline didn't give orders like this. She didn't have to. And the defiance he perceived lingering like a brick wall beneath her calm exterior told him she was nowhere near ready to back down. Frankly she seemed on the verge of breaking a sweat—and she'd never done that before, either. Jovians didn't perspire.

"Jimmy can get there a lot faster than I can. Send him. I'll follow as soon as I can," he told her.

Maybe if Jimmy went, Caroline would relax a little. That is, if she could catch up to him.

She eased back and raised her chin. "Fine. Let me know when you want to leave, and I'll make the arrangements myself."

12

A s soon as Caroline left with her clones, Evander headed into the garden room and observed the live feed coming from Philly. Across the green that made up Independence Lawn, the humans carried signs that read, "We don't need you" and "Stay in your place," while the clones, dressed in the black pants and T-shirts of typical security attire, manned the perimeter surrounding the venue. Each one of them was so fit and calm that their unified silence left a menacing impression. They didn't need to carry signs in order to make a scene. The footage of them walking the streets toward Liberty Square earlier that afternoon reeked of intention: they were too professional, too neatly aligned to appear benevolent. They couldn't help but resemble soldiers marching battalion-style to war.

The problem was the humans *did* need them. They needed them to continue to do what they did, to guard and protect. The clones played an important role. *Now I really sound like a Jovian*, he thought. But it was true. Humans needed the clones whether they liked it or not. Because Earth would one day be attacked, possibly soon. He didn't know what "soon" meant to the Jovian elite, in this case—whether a month or ten years, or longer. Either way, humans alone would not have the strength or know-how to overcome an outer-space entity of the sort David and Jimmy seemed to expect.

Evander's phone beeped a text.

I want to meet with you.

An unknown number.

Since leaving office, he'd had the same cell number shared only with immediate family members and a few others, like President Abela. According to secret service protocol, if someone unknown contacted him, he was to tell Elsa or Martin immediately. Before Evander replied, the texter was back with a second message.

I speak for the clones. My name is Drew, short for Andrew, as in a clone of your father, but I'm sure you've already figured that out. I'm the one who slept with your mother. That practically makes us family.

Evander felt his face contort into something of a snarl. He stood and crossed the garden room, telling Nadia he had to take care of something. Then he continued out the door, into the backyard. As he followed the path toward the patio, he read the texts again. He knew of a clone named Drew, and knew that he'd lived for a very short time with Svetlana. Evander wasn't sure how to respond. In the meantime, Drew sent another text.

Okay, so we didn't sleep together, but we shared a bed. I worked for your grandmother until six months ago. It's in your best interest to respond to me.

Either this was a prank, or the guy was a fool. Maybe he's just a guy with a dumb sense of humor. Either way, Drew seemed no match for a former president practiced in the art of negotiation. How did he even get this number? The texts continued to come in.

You're the only leader I'll talk to.
Are you there?
Hello?
Do I have to ply you with flattery before you'll engage?
I know you have a soft spot for humans.
Will you meet with me?
I assure you it's in your best interest.

Evander finally replied, *Yes.*

You can bring your two secret service friends, but no one else. I'm picking the place.

Elsa would never agree to that.

That depends, Evander typed. *Where do you want to meet—and when?*

At 4:40 a.m. the following morning, Evander, Elsa, and Martin pulled into a street-side parking space about half a block away from the meeting place, a coffee and Danish shop on the outskirts of Philadelphia. Called Cup of Joe, its hybrid owners were entrenched in the movement.

While Evander and Martin waited in the van, Elsa first peered through the large front window of the shop, then waited for a young, strapping Leo clone to open the door.

Evander sensed no danger as Elsa swept the shop's interior and soon signaled Martin with the all clear. She met them on the sidewalk in front. "One rear exit," she said, for Martin's benefit. "Three guards. The target is at a table on the left when you walk in."

"He's not a target," Evander said. "Please don't shoot him."

"Yes, we'll see," she responded, no hint of joking. Evander sensed some lingering disappointment on her behalf around the fact that he'd set this meeting without getting her go-ahead first.

The three of them entered the shop. Not scheduled to open for another hour or two, the place stood empty of baristas and servers, the Closed sign dangling lopsided from a hook on the front door. Evander had promised Drew thirty minutes.

One of Drew's fellow clones, a Miranda, followed them inside. Martin moved to the back of the building beside the Leo, almost twice his girth.

Drew seemed somewhat out of place in his black-on-black security uniform, sitting with an ankle propped upon his knee as if this were the most casual of meetings. He appeared to be about thirty in age, which probably meant he was older. The Andrew clones aged more slowly than ordinary humans.

Evander stepped in, observed café-style tables and chairs, the usual French presses for decoration and shelves with well-used books. "Nice place," he said.

Drew gave it a once-over as if just then noticing the surroundings. "Yeah, I like it."

"So where's your coffee?"

"I only like the smell," Drew said without missing a beat. "Never drink the stuff cause it gives me a stomachache. I'm sure it affected your father the same way." He gestured to the chair in front of him. "Please have a seat."

Evander stared. He knew how intimidating a good stare could be. "I doubt you're much like my father was." Then he sat.

"Your mother didn't think so either," Drew said. "Which I find weird considering I have his DNA."

"Right. If you knew anything about the science behind cloning, you'd realize temperament is only partly determined by genetics. Where you were born, the circumstances, the care you did or did not receive as a child all play into it in a significant way."

"Well, I came to be in the bowels of Starbright. For a long time, I was Caroline's No. 1, as I'm sure you already know." Drew spoke without shame and with an air that hinted at enjoyment in dispensing these facts. "But I'm not here to talk about your grandmother or my upbringing. And I want you to know I harbor no ill will toward your mother. On the contrary, she gave me the best advice I've ever received from anyone human, Jovian, or clone."

"And that was?"

"She said I should think for myself."

Evander didn't try to camouflage his pride. "Sounds like her."

"For most, a comment like that may not have triggered a revelation, but for this clone, it did. "

"You started the movement?"

"I did. Along with a few like-minded others."

"Okay," Evander said. "Well, the situation is growing rapidly more dangerous, as you know."

"I regret the accidents that have occurred. But the clones won't take responsibility for the deaths. It's our right to voice our concerns and bring awareness to them. We didn't ask the humans to oppose us, and we certainly didn't kill them."

Evander paused before answering. "You do realize you've created a highly emotional situation. Humans don't sit back when they feel threatened, and more clones gather daily. You *look* like an army out there."

"We look how we have always looked."

"You're frightening the human population. Isn't that obvious?"

Drew shrugged. "Fear is good for exposure."

Evander sat back. He didn't think fear was good for anything. Fear made everything worse. Had Drew not studied the history books?

"My interest, as always, is to keep the peace," Evander said. "I'm sure you know that."

"Yes, I do. And I admire you for it. But sometimes in order to take a step forward, the peace must be sacrificed."

"What is it you want?" Evander asked.

Drew's face grew sober, his playful gleam flamed out. "It's simple, really. My people want equality."

Evander allowed the statement to settle between them. After a moment, he said, "I've gathered that much from the protests."

"You want details. Of course. I've got plenty of them. First off, we're tired of living in the humans' shadows. For two generations now we've been told what to do, what to think, who we can be. You worry about humans because they're not as intelligent or strong or talented as clones, but in the meantime, *we're* the oppressed. Shackled by society's standards. That was fine in the beginning, when there were just a few of us sprinkled around Kirksberg. When the only clones came from your and your father's DNA. But we're everywhere now. Clones made from your extended family and the hybrids made from your and your father's clones live in every town in this great nation and, to a lesser but growing degree, in nations throughout the world. In the years to come, we'll be the prevalent species. I think you're well aware of that."

Evander held Drew's stare, denying him a response.

"Okay," he said, with a shrug. "Well, we want to be allowed to think for ourselves. We want *real* lives. Is that so hard to understand?"

"You *have* real lives," Evander said.

"What we're living is a life that was chosen for us. Your family decided this is what we would be. But we don't want to work security and become police and be your armed forces anymore."

"I understand. But minds are hard to change. Whatever I can do to help you and your cause, it will take time. Things are improving, I assure you. The hybrids are getting ahead. They're leading the way for all clones."

Drew raised one hand, his impatience showing in the corners of his downturned mouth. "We all know the clones who have bred themselves into the population are doing fine and dandy, and that's nice for them. Some of them aren't joining us in this fight, and I get it. On the other hand," he said, his voice growing in volume, "the clones Caroline kept for herself, the ones bound to her and the royalty, *they're* my people. Those who have joined the armed forces and security jobs throughout this once-violent country are my people, too."

"I understand," Evander said, thinking, *I tried to tell Caroline. All along I tried to change her mind.* "Who else have you spoken with? Besides me, I mean."

"I've spoken to your grandmother many times over the years. I warned her this would be a problem. She didn't think so. Like you, I'm Jovian, so until recently I thought I didn't need to speak in order to be heard. But more and more each day I feel like the clones are being cut off from the oneness. Am I right about that?"

"Actually, communications have been difficult for all Jovians."

Drew's brow arched with surprise. "How convenient."

"As a matter of fact, until two days ago, I thought I was the only one who could no longer hear," Evander confessed.

"Huh." Drew pressed his lips together and observed Evander for an elongated moment, most likely in search of evidence that he was lying. "You've made a good show of faith, coming here, meeting with me. Now do me one better."

"That depends. What do you want?"

Drew moved closer, his hands on the table, head leaned

in. "Tell Caroline we won't live like this anymore. We want jobs that we choose to do. We want fair pay for our work. We want humans to stop treating us like second-class disposables, like it doesn't matter whether we live or die on the job."

Evander nodded. "When I was in office, I created equal rights legislation that applies to all human beings—"

"I'm not talking about legislation," Drew said, sitting up, "and I think you know that."

"But it's a good start," Evander said. "It will take time, granted, but I believe we'll get to a place where both humans and clones live happily together, equally, side by side. You have my word that I won't stop fighting until they do."

Drew laughed as if thinking him a poor, misled child. "I'm sorry," he said, "because I know you mean well, but the clones can't wait for some piece of paper you signed to take shape in the real world. A war is coming, and from what our intelligence has gathered, the opponent is impregnable."

He grinned wryly, as if to say, *That's right. I know big words and I use them properly.*

Evander placed an elbow on the table and leaned forward. "I don't doubt your intelligence, Drew, but nothing that involves humans happens quickly. Revolutions, violent or not, require time to play out."

"That's not my problem," Drew said with sudden abruptness. "We want change now. It's a matter of survival for humans, Jovians, clones, dogs, cats, squirrels—all of us."

"You said a war is coming," Evander said. "What opponent are you referring to specifically?"

"The one from Io."

"Io?" Evander suffered a pain in the middle of his head, and he clenched his fists to withstand it. A harsh shriek as powerful as a rushing train entered his mind, whooshing through with a blast that seemed to shout his name in some strange electronic language.

Drew's chair whined across the floor as he made room between them. "His eyes are rolling back!" he shouted.

Elsa swooped in, a stony look of ready-to-kill on her face. Evander raised his hand and tried to tell her he was all right, but the bizarre phenomenon tore through his brain. *E-vander*, the voice called, rippling through in echoing waves, then growing faint before a gust of wind seemed to blow it away.

Up close, Elsa's eye crystals sparkled. She was ready to take him to the floor, he knew, prepared to begin CPR, should it be necessary. "It's okay," he managed, as he tried to blink his way back to normalcy. "I'm okay," though he didn't know if he was.

Drew's hands remained raised in surrender. "I didn't touch him, you know that, right?"

"I'll kill you if you ever do," Elsa said, her voice slicing the air like a blade. "Back up farther."

He obliged, and she returned her attention to Evander, still seated in the chair. "Are you all right, Mr. President?"

The pain vanished along with the unusual sounds. Whatever visited him had come and gone in a flash, and he breathed as if he were winded. "I'm fine. Just a sudden . . . migraine." He knew it wasn't a headache. Someone had tried to reach him, but who?

"Martin. Water," Elsa barked, still observing Evander with intensity.

Martin placed the cold bottle in Evander's hand.

"Thank you. I'm good, Elsa. You can," he coughed, "go back to where you were." He put on a purposely placid expression.

"I'll be the judge of that." She grabbed his wrist to monitor his pulse. "One-twenty-three over eighty-one, ninety-two beats per minute."

"He said he's fine," Drew grumbled. "Calm down."

Elsa's white hair whipped around and slapped her cheek as she turned to scowl at Drew. "I told you to back the hell up. Do I have to make you shut the hell up as well?"

"Okay, Elsa. Thank you." Evander dipped his head in the direction she'd come from, gesturing for her to return.

Drew squinted, beaming a mix of humor and hatred. "You think I'm just a stupid clone, don't you?"

"*She's* a hybrid," Evander said, "and AI, so I highly doubt that."

Drew remained intrigued. "The hybrids I know don't generally think about killing as a means of retribution."

Obviously Drew hadn't met those trained for the secret service. "Okay, Elsa," Evander repeated. "Give us just a few more minutes."

She touched his forehead. "Ninety-eight point five. Are you sure?" she said.

He nodded.

She stared at him a moment longer, then with measured steps returned to her post. Martin retook his place adjacent to the back door.

Evander gestured Drew forward. "Please excuse the interruption. Continue what you were saying."

Drew inched toward the table. "Are you sure? I don't want to be blamed for whatever is going on with you."

"You were saying you believe Earth will be attacked?"

"Yes, it will. And the Jovians are going to expect the clones to defend it. There are still some clone loyalists who will do that, but not near enough to get the job done. My people won't help without a promise of a free and fair future from Caroline, Edmund, David, the highest in this royal nest of Jupitarians. And I'll tell you something else, if the Jovians don't provide that promise, and the humans don't get on board with this program, they won't have a chance against this foe. And we'll sit back and watch them perish. I promise you, we will."

Drew just admitted the Jovian oneness wasn't working for clones, so how did he even know out about the attack? Someone must have leaked the information.

"What do you know about this impregnable opponent?" Evander said.

"It's wild, chaotic, unpredictable." Drew opened a tin of mints and popped one into his mouth. "You know what unintelligent species are like." He held out the tin. "Want one?"

"No, he does not," Elsa spoke loud and clear from across the room.

Evander answered with a quick shake of his head. "Most of them don't space travel."

Drew raised his brows. "Not the way you or I might, but there are other ways."

"Are you saying they'll fly as a group like geese migrating across the galaxy."

"That's one possibility."

"Why haven't we heard of these creatures before? Why haven't our travelers seen them, or warned us?"

"Maybe they tried to but failed. Communications are down. You said so yourself."

"Then how did you get your information?"

"We have something of a secret weapon, I guess you could call it." Drew looked over his right shoulder and said, "Connie."

Evander leaned forward, eyes squinting as he scanned the left side of the room. He saw nothing out of the ordinary: a space with tables and chairs, a few pieces of wall art, a shelf with an assortment of coffee mugs—but then some movement grabbed his attention, and Elsa lunged, apprehending a body that had seemingly appeared out of thin air.

"She's not dangerous," Drew said, loudly. "Or armed."

With Elsa pulling both of her arms behind her back, a woman came into view. *Had she been there the whole time?* Connie? She stood at five feet tall, just like old Aunt Constance, but her features didn't mesh with Constance's elderly features. No glasses, first of all, and her smooth skin and angular face led Evander to believe she was the equivalent of twenty-year-old. Her brown hair reached her shoulders, unlike Constance's short cut.

Elsa held the young woman, who didn't struggle.

"You can let her go now," Drew demanded.

"Who are you?" Evander asked her. "How did you get in here?"

She spoke with confidence, no element of anger involved: "I go by Connie. I'm Jovian. A clone of your aunt's."

There was something strange about her. Something intangible. The whole of her blurred around the edges. The sensation made Evander's eyes feel numb, and he stifled the urge to rub them.

"Let her go," Evander told Elsa, who did as he said, though not until she'd thoroughly patted the woman down.

Connie took a few slow steps toward them and sat in a chair two tables away.

Everyone knew that Constance had cloned herself. What they didn't know (or, at least, what Evander hadn't known) was that she'd taken cloning a step further and gave this one a special talent. Why wasn't he surprised? In spite of her quiet, unobtrusive, grandmotherly ways, Aunt Constance was the one who had used Uncle Jimmy's lab work to perfect the cloning process. She'd duplicated not only Andrew and Evander but went on to make the Leos and Mirandas. And because she was a narcissist, like some of the Jovian elite seemed to be, she'd also made a special clone of herself. One that went unnoticed, apparently.

"You've been here all along?" Evander asked.

Connie sat with her arms straight at her sides, the same way Aunt Constance often did. "Information gathering is a talent I have," she said softly.

"Does Constance know you've joined Drew?"

"No. No one knows. I was a special project. Caroline may not even be aware that I exist."

That's interesting, Evander thought. *Also, improbable. And why would Constance make a special clone without Caroline's knowledge?*

"Don't feel bad for not seeing her," Drew said. "She's all but invisible."

"So you've been eavesdropping," Evander passed Drew a look. "That's how you get your information?"

"Connie is co-leader of the movement. She knows everything I know."

"You should have told me she was present."

"I paid Caroline a visit last week," Connie said before Drew could answer. "She's not too happy with you."

"I'm aware," Evander said. "Do you think she's behind the species that will attack?"

"If she is, I didn't hear her say anything about it."

"What did you hear her say?"

"Just what Drew told you."

"So, now that this is all clear to you—" Drew chimed in as Evander's black van pulled up to the coffee shop.

"Nothing is clear to me yet."

"Then let me sum up in simple terms," Drew said. "Earth will be attacked. The clones won't defend the planet unless the Jovians provide a promise of our future freedom, the same rights humans enjoy and take for granted every day of their lives."

"And?"

"That's it. Take the message to them. Your wife is human

and your children may as well be, so you have some pretty high stakes in this. I trust you'll do the right thing."

The remark about his children struck a protective nerve. "I'll tell Caroline and the others," Evander said, "but you have to do something for me, too. Stop encouraging the violence in Philadelphia."

"Clones haven't committed any violent acts—"

"Do what you can to prevent future violence. Do I have your word on that?"

"You have *my* word," Connie said.

"Thank you," he said with a nod.

"Fine. You have my word as well," Drew said. "The way I see it, all we have to do is tell the humans about the attack. They'll recognize how much they need us, and humans and clones will band together to fight the bigger enemy."

He isn't wrong, Evander thought.

But somehow it seemed too simple.

13

The following morning, as Fran and Max arrived for work through Starbright's back entrance, Fran thought about the meeting with Leo and how he'd gone home not knowing what Caroline might do about Leonard's punch. Fran wasn't sure whether he should be pissed at himself or disappointed in the squad, or what. Should he have argued that in the grand scheme of things one punch was a very minor offense? He knew that wouldn't get him far. The Jovians were all about nonviolence, the zero-tolerance policy. Maybe he should have offered his resignation. But he didn't want to quit. He liked his job. He was great at it, or had been until recently.

Still, it was just one punch.

He probably did the right thing by sucking it up, but this feeling of not-knowing bothered him. He'd never suffered bouts of indecision back when he wore the FBI badge. Back then his instincts led him well. He took risks without considering them risks, ready to sacrifice himself for his team, or whomever he protected, without a second thought. The fact that he'd lost his arm trying to save a young recruit had proved that much.

And then, a few years later, Svetlana returned to Kirksberg and the Jovians somehow grew his arm back, neglecting to explain how, as was their way. Svetlana took off in a spaceship destined for a different time and universe, and the Jovians hired Fran as head of security. In that way, they'd helped him get his family back, and more than that, his life.

He couldn't help but feel like he owed them.

Anyway, new day, fresh slate. In the comms room, as Fran booted up computers, Max plunked into a chair and hunched over his cell phone, playing one of his fighter pilot games like it was the most pressing responsibility in the world.

"Put that away. Anyone sees you with that thing in your hand, you *will* be fired."

The kid's disgruntled scowl accused him of betrayal. "You never said what Leo wanted yesterday."

"Oh, nothing. No worries. We need to get to work. Gotta get this problem in the planetarium under control."

"What, the 'distant buzzing sound' again?" Max mocked with finger quotes in the air. "Old lady's probably got a fly stuck in her head."

"Actually, I heard it too. Remember? I thought it might be a bug of the spying sort. But nothing has turned up." Fran picked up a pencil and spun it around in his right hand. "Has to be in the wiring—or maybe the software." He cocked a glance at Max. "You know anything about software?"

"I've checked the electronic systems in this room twice already, and I'm pretty sure whatever you're hearing has nothing to do with software." He pulled a how-dumb-are-you face, and Fran chuckled, then swatted the back of Max's head.

As if sensing the potential for violence, Caroline appeared in the doorway.

Fran hadn't heard the door open and did a double-take before he realized she was actually standing there.

"Frances," she said in an almost-friendly way.

He didn't find her as off-putting as Svetlana always had, but he wouldn't describe her as soft and cuddly, either. Her presence brought with it the electrical buzz that set his hair on literal edge, and he wouldn't have been surprised to learn electricity rather than blood ran through her veins.

The only person who called him Frances was his mother, and she'd died when he was in college. Needless to say, the utterance of his full name did the job of getting his attention.

"Yes, ma'am," he said and he stood up, as he always did in her presence.

"Leonard has been promoted. You and he are now co-leaders of the security squad."

Damn it! He knew there'd be fallout for that stupid punch. But this? Leonard *promoted*?

"I've already told him," she continued, "and I expect a smooth transition on both your parts."

A voice from inside Fran objected strenuously. But like a diver who tries to speak underwater, the words remained below, encapsulated in air bubbles. "Yes, ma'am."

She crossed her arms over her chest and shifted her attention to Max, still seated when he should have been standing. "Hello, Max," she said, leaning forward with curiosity.

"Stand, Max," Fran ordered.

The kid suffered some kind of spasm as he floundered up, his skinny legs seemingly twisted together, bumping the chair with enough force to push it over behind him. "Sorry, sorry," he said. "Yes, ma'am. I mean, good morning, ma'am." The chair's metal legs rattled as he struggled to right it.

Caroline's ominous gaze remained fixed on Max for another tortuous moment before she returned her attention to Fran. "I'm wondering if you think the sound I've detected might indicate interference of some sort," she said.

"Interference?"

"Something magnetic within the ceiling or ductwork, perhaps?"

He found himself nodding, though he was no scientist and had no clue about magnetic forces nor where they came from or whether they could be blamed for unexpected sounds.

"I'd like you to search for a magnetic field on the property at large."

"Right. Of course, we'll check it out," he said, worried her cold stare might turn his skin blue.

"Please make that determination before the end of the week and report your findings to Leo."

"I will," he said, and then added, "thank you" for no other reason than right now, in front of his clumsy, game-playing son, Caroline intimidated the hell out of him worse than any FBI authority ever had.

Finally she walked away in her fitted skirt and blouse made of whatever expensive fabric that was, well practiced in her high heels, looking like her plan was to stun the paparazzi on New York's Fifth Avenue as soon work got out.

He turned back to Max, feeling like he'd just been through the wringer. "Could this week get any worse?"

Max gave him a lackluster shrug.

"Never mind," Fran said. "I already know the answer."

14

In the van on the way back from the meeting with Drew, Evander considered a national campaign for clones. He'd have to get a proposal together before speaking to President Abela, which meant he needed to gather ideas and draft a speech.

It would be a humanitarian campaign espousing civil rights and the push for fair and humane treatment of clones. The problem, as he saw it, was that many humans couldn't see the world from another individual's perspective, couldn't walk a day in someone else's shoes. If they could, they would realize clones were just as human as they were. Not fakes and disposables but thinking, loving, hoping individuals, just like themselves. . . .

Getting them to acknowledge this wouldn't be easy. They liked having the clones to protect them. They liked thinking it wasn't a big deal when a clone died in the line of duty. It was more comfortable for them to accept that a fake person had died in place of a real one. Getting them past this lie would be difficult.

In order to deflate the growing tension between humans

and clones, Evander would have to change minds. Change human behavior. And that was easier said than done.

It would begin with something simple. Something the human mind could easily grasp.

The speech would begin with a *story*. Which story that would be, he hadn't yet decided.

Evander grabbed his cell, commanding, "Voice memo," before he began to speak:

"Society can be judged on the way it treats its children, elderly, animals—and clones."

He expected to hear a few angry cries and taunts at this point.

"By now you are familiar with this statement because you've heard me say it many, many times. Granted, the addition of 'clones' is new to the list. And in my opinion, it's been a long time coming."

That wasn't a bad start. He continued to work, forgetting about Elsa and Martin, who rode side-by-side with him in the van.

After a time, he gazed out the window and recognized the neighbor's front lawn, then felt the pull of the van's turn into the drive. They were home. "End voice memo," he said.

The van came to a halt as Evander admired the spring plants and how they resembled pools of living color—and then the front door of his house burst open and Nadia flew through. Her wild eyes told him something awful had happened. Habit made him clear his mind and attempt to tap into the Jovian oneness—but doing so led to a mere murmur of indistinguishable voices.

The van's door slid back with an automatic whoosh.

"What happened?" he said.

"She's gone. I can't find her. It's not like her to hide from me." Nadia looked like she'd traveled through a wind tunnel: hair blown back, sweater off one shoulder, eyes watery.

"Natasha? When did you see her last?"

"She was in her bedroom upstairs. I was in the kitchen. I didn't hear her come down. Someone must have taken her. She wouldn't have left, not without telling me."

He watched her struggle to remain strong, her thin arms wrapping around herself as a means of keeping it together.

"What about your team? Not one of them saw her leave?"

"They're searching the house and the yard. They can't find her. We've been through the house twice," she said, voice cracking.

"You didn't call me."

"They told me you were already on your way."

While Elsa and Martin joined the search, Evander drew Nadia in, her body becoming lost in his embrace as he absorbed her terror as best he could. It burned like a fever in his chest, then when she moved out of his reach, blew like ash in the open air.

"Maybe she fell asleep somewhere," he said. "Under Dmitri's bed, or in the—"

"She also may have passed out somewhere," Nadia said, with a tortured look. A sudden spate of tears spilled over her cheeks. She wiped them and said, "Her heart," her chin quivering.

"I'm sure she's fine," he said, as they entered the house together. "I would know."

In the past he would have said so with 100 percent confidence, but since the oneness had been corrupted, he couldn't know anything for sure. Natasha was still so young. She'd never spoken to him using the oneness—each Jovian came to it in their own time and to his knowledge, she'd not yet arrived. Still, better to give Nadia some solace, even if it weren't true.

"Where's Dmitri?" he said.

"In the garden room. With Eliot. I'll check on him."

"Did you look in her closet?" He took the stairs three at a time. "Sometimes she sleeps in there."

"I did."

On his own now, Evander sped through the bedrooms on the second floor, passing Martin, who made eye contact before shaking his head. He continued up the narrow staircase to the attic, where a platform opened to three separate rooms with low, angular ceilings. Fun places for a little girl to play or hide. Though, Natasha wasn't the sort to hide, especially if she heard people calling her name.

But maybe she had passed out. Anything was possible.

"Where are you, baby girl?" he said. Hunched over so he wouldn't bump his head on the low ceiling, he opened the door to the room on the left first. Who was he kidding? The secret service had been over the house twice already.

He pulled his phone from his back pocket and commanded it to message Drew. *Where is she?* he dictated as he stepped around boxes of Nadia's ball gowns and his formalwear, and shined the cell's light into dark corners.

Thirty seconds passed. No answer from Drew. He closed the door and approached the central room, a small dormer space with storage. Boxes and more boxes.

The dots that indicated an impending text appeared.

Drew: *You'll have to be more specific.*

Evander: *My little girl. You had someone take her while I was at the meeting. Another invisible Connie, maybe.*

Drew: *No. I did not. And there's only one Connie as far as I know.*

Evander: *I already agreed to help you. There was no reason for this. Kidnapping a former president's daughter is a serious offense—*

Drew's next text interrupted. *I'm not stupid enough to do that.*

Evander grumbled, then wrote, *You better not be.*

I just asked you for a favor. Drew texted back, and then: *Why would I?*

He was right. It didn't make sense.

Drew: *Have you spoken to your grandmother? Sounds like something she would do.*

Evander wanted to protest, and nearly did, but he hesitated, and in that hesitation, instinct told him Drew might be right.

A moment later, another text followed: *Good luck finding her. Let me know if the clones can help.*

Evander clicked off his cell. Drew was right. Caroline had kidnapped Svetlana and himself when he was an infant. She could be behind it. He'd been cut off from the family oneness, and maybe this was why. Maybe Caroline, who'd become more and more secretive over the months, slowly but surely snuffed out the oneness just for this reason. But why would she kidnap Natasha? What would that accomplish?

"Call Caroline," he told his phone.

A woman's voice answered, "Caroline's phone."

"It's Evander. I need to speak to her."

"Oh, hi, Evander. It's Miranda. She's not available, but I'll be happy to pass on a few words."

"No," he said. "I need to speak to her."

No reply.

"It's an emergency, Miranda."

"Is it, though?" she asked.

Of all the Jovians, Miranda was the only one of the elite who used sarcasm as well as any human. But now was not the time.

"This isn't a game," Evander said.

"Caroline doesn't need a phone to speak to people, least of all you. And she doesn't know where your daughter is, so even if there is an emergency, it's not one we can help you with. Will that be all?"

The scathing heat of anger pulsed through Evander's veins. He'd never felt such searing emotion. It was a rare moment in which he wanted to harm another individual. "In the name of my mother, if you don't hand the phone to—" He didn't get to finish the thought.

"Yes, Evander. What is it I can help you with?"

It was Caroline. He drew a shaky breath and tried to remember why he'd called.

"My daughter," he said. "Natasha is missing."

"I'm sorry to hear that."

She didn't sound sorry—and he wanted to know why.

"What do you know about it?" he said.

Met with background noise and nothing more, he wondered if she still held the phone to her ear.

"Caroline, my daughter is missing. I'm asking you if you know anything about it."

"It's not what you think," she said.

"Do you even know what I think? Can you hear my thoughts?"

"Some, yes. Enough to know that you're quite upset."

"Where is my daughter?"

"I haven't taken her. If someone has, I don't who it is. I haven't learned anything about it. I can ask David to investigate, but he's not hearing the way he once did. If he knew, I would know."

If Caroline didn't take Natasha, and Drew hadn't taken her, where was she? Could it be that some random disgruntled American kidnapped her? Evander had received death threats throughout his twelve years as commander in chief, but only a smattering since he'd left office six months ago. Then again Elsa and Martin never failed to remind him how many people didn't care for the way he'd led the mission to heal the Earth. Still, this didn't feel like a human act. The secret service could prevent a kidnapping from occurring 99 percent of the time.

It had to be Jovian. Someone Natasha knew.

Evander was pretty sure Uncle Jimmy had left the planet by now, even if Jimmy didn't take Caroline's advice to go to Io. He no longer sensed Jimmy's presence, though Evander didn't know if he could trust his senses at this point. But if he was right and Jimmy had gone, that left David, Leo, or Aunt Constance. Leo wouldn't know what to do with a child, and David was in no shape to pull off a kidnapping. Sweet, old-lady Constance could have done it. She created an invisible clone on the sly, after all. Still, Evander doubted she'd be able to convince Natasha, who'd never met her before, to leave home without telling her mother. Maybe Miranda? She could pull it off, but would she want to? He couldn't see Miranda tolerating a child's near-constant needs. And Caroline wouldn't waste Miranda's time with such an assignment —she needed Miranda at her side.

Maybe, as Nadia feared, Natasha had collapsed somewhere. Maybe on the playground or running to a friends' house. The thought of her lying in the dirt, injured and alone, leaned heavily on his own heart. *She has to be all right. I would know if she wasn't, wouldn't I?*

"Call me if you learn anything. Please," he said.

"In the meantime, I'll send the security squad to help." For twelve years, she'd been urging him to use her security squad instead of the secret service.

"Kind of you. But we'll be fine. I'll let you know when we find her."

He was about to hang up when he remembered the meeting with Drew.

"Caroline, wait. There's something else. The clones. The

situation in Philadelphia. I spoke with one of their leaders, and I'm of the opinion that we need to take them seriously."

He paused to allow her time to respond. Seconds ticked by, and she said nothing.

"And whatever truce we come to," he added, "is going to require your cooperation."

Again, he waited for her response.

"But I can't talk now," he said, not knowing what else to do. "Maybe we can talk more tomorrow, if we find Natasha. I have to go."

"Evander?"

"Yes?" he said, hopeful for what she might say.

"It's in your best interest to trust me. Remember that."

15

W hen Leo called asking for a team to help out at Evander's residence, Fran volunteered himself and Max, thinking it would be a good way to keep Max a safe distance from Leonard and any other disgruntled clones. He recruited two of his best non-clone squad members to join them: Jake and Shonda, both as professional as they come. Climbing the stairs to the Peterman residence, he rang the bell expecting the secret service to answer. When Evander materialized instead, his nerves suffered a power surge that caused the muscles in his face to tense and quiver. His arms hung numbly at his sides, and his tongue stuck to the roof of his mouth.

This kind of anxiousness ventured far beyond his normal.

Of course he'd met Evander in the past. He'd met him when Evander was a baby in Svetlana's arms. But that was over twenty-five years ago. This middle-aged adult who stood before him—this *former president*, no less—might as well have been a complete stranger, not to mention one of the most powerful human beings in the world. A swooping swell of intimidation swept through his already-agitated body.

He fought back the flood of insecurity with the remembrance that he'd been the one to help Svetlana hang on to the infant Evander way back when David showed his true alien self in the Kirksberg Park. A full-fledged FBI agent at the time, Fran had stuck by Svetlana and found a way for her to raise Evander in Russia.

Twenty-five years seemed like a lifetime ago. And now, due to the strange way Evander had aged, the baby was a middle-aged man, same as Fran.

Fran stepped forward. "Nice to see you. I'm Fran Vasquez."

Evander grabbed his hand with unexpected strength and loads of authority. His eyes pierced Fran's vulnerable place. That unusual blue-green, just like Andrew's. Fran couldn't take the intensity of the moment and sought out the floor, if only for a second.

"Good to see you again," Evander said with only a trace of a smile—because his little girl was missing and this was not a social visit, so *pull yourself together,* Fran scolded himself.

He and Evander had met as employees of Starbright just one time about five months before. A chance encounter in the corridor in which Evander and his entourage bustled past. At the time, Fran had shaken Evander's hand and backed the hell away without uttering a word. Before he even knew whether Evander had recognized him, the secret service woman with the white hair and pantsuit to match had whisked the former president off to whatever meeting he was late for.

And now this strange sense of familiarity and history materialized between them, as if Svetlana herself somehow had willed this meeting to occur.

As Fran's thoughts lingered on Svetlana, Max nudged him forward, whisper-shouting, "Dad!"

Evander had walked away, and they were meant to follow. Without Jake and Shonda, apparently, because those two stayed put.

Fran and Max passed through the foyer into the kitchen, then through another, shorter hallway and into a sizable room with bright white walls encased in wood, the backyard's lawn and flowers and plants sprawling beyond the windows like a public park. . . . On the opposite side of the room, Evander's son lay on his back on the carpet, staring upward at what appeared to be a set of keys he raised above his head. He was making strange utterances that no one seemed to notice. *What was his name?* Fran could never remember. Something Russian that started with a D. . . . *D. D. Dmitri!*

Even from this distance, Fran recognized the boy's resemblance to Svetlana.

President Peterman's children were kept out of the limelight and photographed seldom, so Fran had never seen them without their faces blurred. Evander and Nadia insisted they remain as anonymous as possible. Who could blame them, with all the talk and speculation, especially when it came to the boy: he was either a genius or the opposite, no one really knew, suffering from chronic illness, possibly muscular dystrophy? Or something like it, something rare, maybe? And the girl . . . *What was it they said about her?* Nothing he could think of. Except that she was young. Maybe kindergarten?

"Isn't that right, Dad?" Max said in a strained voice once again. "President Peterman just asked if you—"

"Please call me Evander," the former commander in chief interrupted as Fran shook out of the pensive whirlwind that had given his focus the wings to fly.

Max conveyed a "don't you dare embarrass me right now" vibe, his fervent brows quivering.

"I'm sorry," Fran said. "It's just . . . overwhelming to . . . " All he could think was, *see your mother's face and your father's eyes in every direction I look*. . . . But no, he couldn't say that. "It's overwhelming to be here with you and your family, Mr. President."

It was the truth, and he wished he hadn't said it aloud, but he didn't know what else to say and had to say something.

What happened next may have only occurred on Fran's end, in his imagination, but it seemed that Evander observed him with a kind of understanding. As if he, too, were thinking of Svetlana and Andrew in that moment— and not only Svetlana and Andrew, but everything that Fran knew about the Jovians, including the spaceship that took Svetlana away, and the travelers, and how Fran made sure that he and his mother made it safely to Russia when he was a baby.

"We don't know each other well but there are years—and miles—of history between us," Evander said, reinforcing what Fran had intuited.

The former president was kind. That much was obvious. Maybe everyone felt that kindness when they met Evander. He came across as an old friend would. Warmhearted, but with the potential to be commanding.

"My mother truly admired you," Evander continued. "If there was anyone in the world we could count on, she said it was you."

Fran's vision blurred and his throat clenched as he fought to stay out of the emotional zone. Determined not to cry— because that would be twice in two days—he bowed his head and concentrated on relieving the pressure in his throat. "Thank you, sir," he said. "I admired her just as much, or more."

Fran half-turned away, getting in a quick throat-loosening cough.

"Oh my God, get a grip," Max said without moving his lips.

Evander reached out and rested a hand on Fran's shoulder. To Fran's surprise, a blanket of calmness came over him. His nerves and sadness dissipated. He wondered if Evander's touch had done something to alleviate the tension, and decided it must have.

Fran snapped into a posture-perfect position and said, "How can we be of best use to you, sir?"

Max retracted his neck, nostrils flaring.

But why? Fran wondered. Had he gone overboard the other way?

Evander acted as if nothing about Fran's behavior was amiss. "The secret service stays very close to me and my family, so it would have been near impossible for someone to abduct Natasha from inside the house or yard. They've canvassed the surrounding neighborhood, but I'd like you to bump out the search even farther." He hesitated for a second or two, then leaned in and spoke softly. "It's not public knowledge, but my daughter has some health issues. She may have wandered, become disoriented or weak. We just don't know."

"I'm sorry," Fran said, doing his best to channel understanding from one parent to another. "We'll take it out as far as you want to go."

"She may be hiding somewhere, or she may be unable to respond to our calls." Evander spoke to Fran directly. "There's also a chance someone she knows has taken her. Who that would be, I'm not sure."

"But your secret service would have seen," Fran said.

"Yes, they should have. And yet here we are."

Is he implying that someone on the inside might be in on it?

The white-haired woman who stood guard like a human hawk came up behind Evander and whispered in his ear.

Evander excused himself and moved away for privacy. He bowed his head and paused to listen as the woman whispered in his ear. Then he raised his head and eyed the agent with the kind of seriousness that changes the consistency of the air in the room. When he returned, he told Fran, "I'll need you and Max to come with me. Tell the other squad members to join the neighborhood search."

With a "yes, sir," Fran took off, hustling through the now-busy kitchen with a staff of five or six he hadn't noticed before. In the foyer, he found Shonda and Jake standing guard at either side of the front door, making themselves useful.

"You two need to search a block out in every direction. Check under every bush, inside every garage and garden shed. Max and I are heading out with the president."

They exited the house, and Fran walked back the way he'd come. Across the room, the sight of Max speaking to the former president, with the male and female secret service listening in, inspired him to move faster. *What the hell can he be saying?*

"I want you and Max in my vehicle, if you don't mind," Evander told Fran as soon as he rejoined them.

"Wherever you need us, sir," Fran said.

Evander walked on with the calm of a world leader because that's what he was.

As they passed through the garden room, Fran wondered where the president's wife was and why Evander would go anywhere with the search for Natasha in full swing. Dmitri appeared to be in his own world, staring at his keys and mumbling, or maybe humming, it was hard to tell which. Fran wondered if Dmitri even knew his sister was missing, if anyone had bothered to ask him if he'd seen her go. And if they did ask, would he be able to answer?

As Fran neared the blanket with the boy on top of it, he noted the kid's pale complexion and dark blue eyes, just like Svetlana's. The resemblance was frightening. Dmitri had her thick brows and head of rich brown hair, her overall coloring. Fran wondered whether he'd inherited her bold spirit as well, then doubted he could have, given the state of his physicality.

As Fran followed Evander and the entourage, rounding the bend that would take him past Dmitri, he hovered momentarily above the boy's skinny body. That's when Dmitri flicked his eyes past the set of keys in his hand and very soberly said, "Hi, Fra-aaan."

Fran's scalp vibrated with electricity so fervently that his vision blurred and the skin on his arms tingled to the point that he felt the need to scratch them. He continued to walk, rubbing his arms and struggling to see clearly, when he stepped on something—the heel of Max's shoe—and Max stumbled as his sneaker flapped and then peeled off.

Fran was still staring at Dmitri as he said, "Sorry, Max, sorry."

Max spun around, his lips pressed so tightly together they disappeared into his mouth. "Crap, Dad," he erupted, "what is wrong with you?" He swiped his shoe from the ground and limped the rest of the way out.

16

In the van, Fran and especially Max seemed starstruck. Evander doubted either of them had ever traveled in such a high-tech vehicle. All of the secret service vans transformed into a compact conference room on wheels, when necessary. Instead of two rows of seats lined up in the usual manner, it provided two facing rows: three seats on one side, three on the other, with armrests and cup holders in between. Small tabletops unfolded from the walls, as needed.

Evander sat in the front center, in between Elsa and Martin, because that was protocol. Across from him, Max and Fran observed. Max picked at the skin on his thumb, and Fran sat straight as a board, on hyperalert.

Evander stared out the window. So far, Fran Vasquez had not lived up to Svetlana's description of "unshakeable superhuman." The guy seemed leery and cautious. Hulkish and clumsy on his feet. Definitely intimidated. Then again, this was their first face-to-face meeting in which they'd had an actual conversation, and plenty of people found it unnerving to speak to the former leader of the free world. Leo had always praised Fran and said how skillfully he handled the security squad, so Evander wouldn't judge.

Funny that Fran's son worked with him.

Maybe *that* was the problem—mixing work with parenting couldn't be easy. Especially when that work proved potentially dangerous. Evander knew how children had a way of chipping away at a parent's self-confidence.

He really wanted to stay home with Nadia and the search party, but President Abela had called for his help, her desperation evident. The tension in Philadelphia had escalated along with the size of the gathering crowd—he'd seen that much on the news. She shouldn't have waited so long to take action. He'd take care of this and then hurry back home. Everything would be all right.

He texted Drew: *On my way to the protest. Will do my best to set things straight.*

Drew: *Still need that promise from your family.*

Evander: *I am aware.*

He slid his phone into the console beside him. To Fran he said, "We're heading into a sizable crowd. Seven to ten thousand, maybe more. It's nothing I can't handle. I know for a fact the clones don't want a fight. But you saw what happened a few days ago. Should it go downhill, get back to the van as quickly as possible."

"Copy that," Fran said, sounding a lot more professional than before.

Elsa moved to respond but then eased back.

"Elsa?" Evander said.

"Specifically, sir, what would you like Mr. Vasquez to do?"

"Keep his finger on the pulse of the crowd. Remain nearby."

"I'll do that, sir," he said. "You can count on me."

The van pulled into a mostly empty lot in the back of Independence Lawn. "We're not leaving until we get clearance," Elsa told them, "so hang tight." She touched her ear, a pensive blankness smoothing her brow as she held fast.

It occurred to Evander that he'd never given a speech of this magnitude without the Jovian oneness at his disposal. A dull gray fog snuffed all sights and sounds as he once again attempted to tap into the secondary consciousness and came up with a hum similar to white noise. He couldn't reach the minds of other Jovians, which meant he wouldn't know what they knew or see what they saw. If there was trouble within the crowd, he wouldn't become aware of it until it was upon him—just like a human wouldn't.

It shouldn't matter, he told himself. *The crowd never knew you had these senses. To them it's no different. They trust you. They won't harm you. You're the only one who knows how vulnerable you feel right now.*

Classical music filtered into the van.

Evander opened his cell phone and brought up the file of his speech. He didn't need to read it again but preferred to do something rather than nothing.

"Follow my lead," Fran spoke in a hushed voice to his son, though Evander heard him with ease.

"Yeah, obviously," Max whispered in reply.

"I've got your back, don't worry."

"Not worried. I thought you were here to protect *him*, not me."

Fran put his hand on his billy club at his side, the pepper spray attached to his belt. He reached into his buttoned shirt and touched the space between inner bicep and chest, most likely checking for the gun he carried in a holster there.

Fran's brows knitted together as he said, "One more thing: do not draw your weapon for any reason."

Max jerked back. "What if—"

"Under no circumstance will you draw your weapon," Fran enunciated.

"I'm security—how is that even possible?"

"It's possible because you'll do as I say," Fran said with steely severity. "Clones don't draw their weapons, security squad don't draw their weapons, and we will not draw our weapons."

"Then why did you tell me to bring it?"

Fran didn't answer right away. "In *only one* circumstance will you draw your weapon."

"Okay, I got it."

"Self-defense."

"Yeah, I got it," Max said, turning to face the window.

Elsa woke from stillness and tapped her upper ear. "Yes, we're here," she said. And then, "They're ready for you, Mr. President."

Evander gave a curt nod. "Let's do this."

Elsa exited the van first, followed by Martin, who knocked the roof a second later. Evander rose from his seat and stepped out the door, putting on his suit jacket and pulling it into form. Fran and Max followed behind him, the four security agents creating a tight perimeter as Evander continued down the cement path toward the entrance to the venue.

Elsa remained a step in front, as usual, with Martin scanning the area as he strode along the right-hand side.

The sound of the crowd grew in strength. A rumbling, vibrating din rose like dust in the aftermath of a meteorite. At first, Evander couldn't make out any words. Even without the oneness he sensed the large number of humans and clones packed into the space. The crowd emitted heat, a hazy humidity that blew toward them as they neared.

And then a vague chant came together out of the cacophony.

"Freedom is a human right! Freedom is a human right!"

The path led to a guarded gate. Tall, muscled men and

women flanked the surrounding eight-foot wall, snapping to attention and moving aside as they became aware of Evander's presence. Elsa approached first. The gate opened. She stood to the side and let Evander pass. The rumble of voices wrapped around them like a snake of sound, thick with the anger and desperation. The chanting once again devolved into a chaotic mess of illegible utterances, some of them coming through in high-pitched hysteria.

Evander would fix this. He had to fix this.

They reached a set of stairs, and Elsa began to climb. She stopped at the top and tapped her ear, her eyes sparkling as she scanned the area. After a moment, she continued the rest of the way up.

Evander recognized the backstage of the amphitheater from when he'd given a speech a year ago. A microphone and podium waited centerstage. When he saw them, the energy within him came to life with wings, a beating heart, and a cresting wave of confidence.

This was what he was made for.

He could handle this.

"All set, sir," Elsa said, as a small entourage moved in their direction, a young woman with waves of black hair at its helm.

Evander recognized President Abela's assistant, Meera. As they shook hands, she softened with relief. "You're here. Thank goodness. Great to see you again, Mr. President. President Abela is thrilled to have you. Can you be ready right away? Is there anything you need?"

"I'm ready when you are," he said.

"Security requires a couple of minutes," Elsa said.

"Of course." Meera put her headset back on. "I'll be right back." She rushed away, four young people following after her, all of them speaking into their cell phones or headsets, whispers of "He's ready" and "All systems go" trailing behind them.

"How long do you plan to speak?" Fran asked Evander.

"Fifteen minutes."

"Whoa," Max said, startling everyone within earshot. "You're going to fix this in fifteen minutes? Dude you are amazing!"

Fran's slow-blink blank stare expressed his desire to be sedated, and Evander empathized with him. Kids always found a way to embarrass their parents, and he supposed the reverse was true as well.

17

F ran and Max left Evander to get a better look at the stage and beyond.

The setup was simple: basically a wide, empty space with a podium for the speaker. That was it. The lawn upon which the crowd stirred and roiled just a few feet below, on the other hand, sent tingles of the fearful sort through Fran's midsection. Evander's lighthearted mood belied the sea of angry humans, some of whom seemed determined to claw their way up the sides of the amphitheater. Fran felt suddenly, horribly out of practice. He could handle a controlled-space situation like the Starbright building any day of the week, but this was a football field–sized public domain filled with highly charged disgruntled beings, all of whom seemed prepared to do battle—in their own way, of course.

Thank goodness we'll be up here and not down there, he thought.

The lawn, situated in the middle of a city square, was the equivalent of a park minus any trees, flowers, or benches.

The clones manned the perimeter as they would at any prearranged protest—raised up on old railroad cars and shipping containers, two or three bodies thick. They appeared calm and organized, and professionally menacing, the polar opposite of the humans, who had worked themselves into a sweaty, boiling lather.

How the hell was Evander going to fix this with one fifteen-minute speech? Fran supposed if anyone could do it, it was Evander.

Plenty of secret service could be found to protect President Abela, as well as Evander, which made Fran wonder why he and Max had been asked to come. Maybe Evander felt he needed a couple of people he knew personally and could trust for reasons other than it was their job to protect him.

"Okay," Fran bent toward Max with the intention of channeling seriousness straight into his brain. "No more bullshit. Treat this like a life-or-death situ—"

The rest of the sentence became lost under the clattering staccato of bellowed orders. "You, take the back, and you, stay in front of that left-hand exit."

It was Leonard. In full Starbright uniform, just like they were.

Why is he here?

"You two," Leonard called to them, "you're on crowd control. Get out there." He jabbed his pointer finger in the direction of the lawn's sea of people.

"No, way." Fran shook his head. "We're on presidential duty at the behest of the former president himself."

Leonard scanned the area, probably in search of Evander, who wasn't nearby. He moved a few steps closer and planted his fists on his hips. "He's a newbie," he said scowling in Max's direction. "That makes him a liability. So, no. I'm not going to let that happen. Get in the crowd. Both of you."

Fran couldn't believe his ears. "*Evander* requested his presence," he said. "You think you can veto an order from the former president?"

Fran started walking away, nudging Max to do the same, but there was a large speaker fencing them in, making the only open path, unfortunately, the one that led to the stage and the crowd beyond.

"Just because you're human doesn't mean you get to pull the nepotism card," Leonard shouted at their backs.

Fran spun around. "The what?" He guided Max to stand behind him. "You can't be serious. He goes wherever I go."

"He's one of us, and he's lower ranking. He belongs in the crowd, where he can do the least harm."

Abela's assistant, the one named Meera, headed toward the podium, then turned leerily toward them, her colleagues following suit as if sensing a fistfight in the making.

At this point, Fran hoped Evander remained out of earshot.

Max said, "It's okay, Dad. I'll go. Don't worry. I know how to follow orders."

"Stay right where you are," Fran said, sure that steam rose from his buzz cut as he sustained Leonard's stare down. "Has your promotion gone straight to your head, Leonard?"

He'd have to talk to Leo about this new arrangement. The partnership obviously wasn't going to work, and it had nothing to do with his own apparent demotion. Fran didn't give two craps about that right now.

Leonard's muscled neck looked ropier than ever. "I'm in charge of this squad just as much as you are. Are you saying I should be quiet? Stay in my lane?"

"That's my kid you want to send out there. He's nowhere near ready for crowd control of this magnitude, and you know it."

"And yet you want him to cover the most revered president this country has ever had?"

With pen in hand, Meera took a step in Leonard's direction. "Excuse me, is there a problem here?"

Fran ignored her effort to get Leonard's attention. At that moment, he couldn't think, see, or hear anything outside of what a huge pain in the ass Leonard had become. "We're staying nearby and covering perimeter like President Peterman asked us to," Fran said, his voice straining under the temptation to go off on him. "So, go do your job and mind your business."

He ran a hand across his forehead, fingers slippery with sweat, then turned slightly to check over his shoulder. Max wasn't there. Fran spun all the way around. Then back again. "Where is he?" he shouted at Leonard. "If anything happens to him today, I swear I will—"

"You mean if anything happens to any of us, don't you? Human or clone?"

"What?"

"Excuse me," Meera shouted this time.

"He went that way." Leonard pointed at the crowd. "At least one of you knows how to follow orders."

With the speaker moved out of the way, Fran took the corridor that led out of the backstage area, hoping to find Max waiting there. When he didn't, he sped down the stairway that descended to the ground. At the bottom, he met with the backs of several mammoth-sized guards. Still, he could see into the crowd beyond them. *Did Max go in there? If so, he couldn't have gotten far.*

Fran passed the guards (who didn't even ask who he was) and breathed in a cloud of sweat. The sound of angry voices swirled like sirens overhead. "Clones go home! Clones go home!" But he didn't hesitate to enter the fray: like a person who jumps into the pool rather than walks in, he joined the thousands on the floor in one fell swoop. Moving forward meant wading in a lagoon of human lava. His angry glare and deep-throated "Out of the way's!" helped him through, but it was slow going.

Why had the kid taken off like that? Just stay behind me. That's all I ask.

The crowd was a many-limbed creature with elbows and knees that bounced off his chest and shins. It also had feet (which he unapologetically stepped on) and asses and other body parts he didn't want to think about rubbing against him with every step. He trudged, a plastic bottle rebounding off his head at one point, as he continued to move forward without hesitation, determined to find Max and get them both out of that pit of flesh and emotion, back to the stage, where they could do the job Evander asked them to do.

Fran reached the halfway mark when he looked up and squinted into the afternoon sun. He worried that he might not find Max, and then he wouldn't be able to keep him safe, let alone stand guard for the former president.

But then, on the far side of the field, clear across the venue, standing on top of one of the old railroad cars, someone whose silhouette matched Max's appeared at the end of a line-up of clones. They were Andrew clones, and their blank stares could easily be mistaken for cocky attitudes.

A young woman, skinny with wild hair, fell into Fran, and he caught her. She shrieked as she continued past. When Fran looked again for Max, the sun had come out from behind some afternoon clouds, and the kid stood out with his mocha-colored skin and small, spindly stature. He looked soft up there. Almost delicate. The worry on his face, obvi-ous. . . . Or maybe that was just how Fran saw him.

How the hell had he crossed the lawn so fast?

"Hey, Max," Fran shouted, bobbing above the crowd as much as he could in an attempt to stand out. "Max!"

The kid didn't notice him—or hear him. He wasn't even facing the crowd, wasn't paying attention. Instead he was turned sideways, speaking to the clone next to him. The clone was showing him something—a tattoo on his forearm—and then Max dropped his head back and . . . *laughed?*

The deeper Fran waded into the mosh pit of humans, the more he realized there wasn't much he and Max, and the perimeter of overlooking clones, would be able to do should the mob turn on Evander. And who was to say the clones would even protect him? Sure, Elsa and Martin would do their job, but would it be enough?

Fran wasn't the kind to abandon his post, and now he was sorry he'd jumped into this crowd, and even more sorry Evander had requested that Max join them on this mission.

The people in this distant part of the lawn screamed louder than the ones up front. They jumped up and down as a group, heavy metal blaring out of several distorted cell phones. Rowdy and laughing. Acting drunk. Like this was some kind of party.

This whole, stupid event was too chaotic for words. *Why the hell did Leonard have to show up?*

The unwieldy squeal of a microphone traveled across the green like a pterodactyl taking flight, the echo of its call filling the startled silence that followed.

The crowd's overall rumble had lowered several decibels.

A woman's voice blasted through speakers fixed to surrounding poles. "Hello, everyone! Hello. We are up and running. Okay, wonderful. This is great. Thank you so much for your patience. Can you hear me? . . ." Tap, tap, clonk. A murmur of a response materialized from the crowd. "I don't know whether you've heard, but someone very special is here to speak with you this afternoon."

Fran continued to push forward, closing in on Max, still yards away.

Damn kid better not move before I get there.

18

Evander stepped up to the microphone and a hushed silence traveled like wind over the unruly crowd. The people closest to the stage closed their mouths and surrendered their attention, as if the sight of their beloved former leader blanketed them in comfort and soothed their hysteria. This was why they had changed the Constitution and allowed him a third term. They loved him, plain and simple.

"It's Evander!" a girl shouted, rising up on her toes before laying back in a trust fall.

Evander paused to take in the roiling sea of people overflowing the too-tight space. The clones, like fence posts, surrounded them in their elevated positions poised on top of shipping containers. *When had they brought those in?* he wondered. No matter, the power he wielded manifested within him in the form of confidence of the highest caliber. It had been a while since he'd been in front of so many, and he snapped into the role the way a vital, missing part snaps into an engine and allows it to purr.

"We love you," a woman near the front screamed, while others deeper within the venue continued to chant: "No clones, clones go home. No clones, clones go home."

Evander raised his arm and waved. "Hi," he said. "It's good to see you all again."

At that, a new chant rode over the others: "Peterman, Peterman, Peterman."

He stepped back and let it continue while he cultivated the calm he would spread like a cloud through the air. It wasn't hard for him to do. He merely concentrated on the task at hand, and his insides began to thrum with warmth. His Jovian DNA provided all he needed to make it happen. People simply felt better about themselves in his presence. Some attributed it to his charisma: he had been dubbed the most charismatic president the people had ever elected. But it was his Jovian DNA that granted him the ability to connect with certain powerful energies he could pull from Earth's atmosphere and beyond. He could reach for the cosmos, so to speak, harness its tranquility, and spread it around.

He returned to the podium and spoke in the voice expected of a president. "Thank you for the warm welcome. I'm here on an important matter, and I'd like to ask your permission to speak on a subject close to my heart and the heart of this nation. It's about you and your neighbors, your friends, and all of the individuals who share this planet."

He did not wait for their permission. The energy gathered within him, and he sent it out. It was like light, a ball of light that corralled inside him and rose through his pores, mingling with air molecules and riding the crests of invisible waves. It spread from himself to his admirers as if through the air they breathed. The most sensitive of humans would wonder what made them feel at peace, and others would sink into repose as if they'd brought it about themselves.

"Not so long ago," he said, "many of you didn't know what a clone was, nor that clones and clone hybrids lived among us. Of course, now you know them as your police, your soldiers, your security guards and officers." He paused. "And you appreciate their work. We all appreciate their hard work."

A man with a beard and a T-shirt ripped from collar bone to armpit shouted, "We were doing fine before they came along, but I don't mind if they want to take a bullet for us. Matter of fact, I've got one for 'em right here." He made a gun of his hand—thumb up, forefinger pointed—and raised it to eye level, sparking those around him to shout a mess of angry, tangled words.

Evander turned in the direction from which the cry originated and raised his hand. "Let's make one thing clear: no one on this bright blue planet is disposable, and thanks to my legislation, you can be interrogated for voicing that suggestion."

Three clones hopped down from their posts and moved at deft speed through the crowd. They snapped handcuffs on the man who'd shouted the sentiment and led him away.

The crowd quieted.

"We all appreciate the work of the clones and hybrids, but protectors are not all that these people are."

Another outcry shattered the peace: "If they don't like it, they can go home!"

"They *are* home," Evander said. "Earth is their home, just like it's yours."

A cheer rose from the front rows, but a dark murmur rumbled in the distance like an ugly aftershock. The clones around the perimeter remained in soldier pose.

Evander continued to gather the internal calm, absorbing its peacefulness and using his mind to dispense it.

"Clones, like humans, have dreams and aspirations.

Strengths and artistic abilities. They care for their families, enjoy earning a living, want to get ahead while contributing to their communities. Just like ordinary humans, not all of them want to solider for this country. Not all of them want to police."

"Equality for clones!" a woman close to the stage shouted and raised her fist. A few other women joined her, and the chant grew in volume. "Equality for clones. Equality for clones."

People throughout the lawn sat back on their heels. No one told the women to shut up. Further and further, the rows of human protesters became still, quiet. The calm was working. They were listening.

"It's a fact that humans and clones up until now have not done a lot of mixing socially. They are different, yet not so different that we haven't been able to get along, not so different that we haven't been able to work side by side. We have proven that we can build relationships when we simply grant each other the opportunity.

"I want you to ask yourself, 'Have I taken the time to get to know the clone who guards my apartment building? The one who makes sure my money is safe? Those who ensure the school my child attends never falls victim to the horrific violence suffered in the previous era?' You do remember that era, don't you? It wasn't so long ago. Maybe twelve years back? Most of you are old enough to know what I'm referring to: the era of violence?"

He continued to speak while concentrating on the calm. It wasn't hard for him. He'd done it for years, changing the minds of the masses while doing what needed to be done to save the planet, to advocate for nonviolence.

He wondered why Abela had waited so long to ask him to speak. And then it occurred to him that it could have been Caroline's influence. She spoke to the president frequently.

The Jovian royalty had forged a secret and direct line to the American presidency ever since citizens voted George Washington into office. And Caroline viewed the clash between humans and clones as a natural part of evolution. Perhaps she'd told Abela to stand down. Perhaps she demanded it.

"We sometimes forget how conflicted the past was. Only twelve years ago, war and murder and violence prevailed. That was the world prior to clones."

The longer Evander sank into the peace of the cosmos, the more the crowd appeared to have submerged in a pool of tranquility. But he hadn't reached them all yet. He could still hear the "clones go home" chant in the distance.

"Many clones will continue to choose to protect because the job suits them. Others will do it because it's the only job they can get. But that needs to change. We must grant clones and hybrids the freedom to make a happy life. We must give them the same freedoms other humans enjoy. We must once again share in an equal way the protection of this great nation.

"There are some who say clones are less outwardly emotional, and perhaps this is true. But less emotional does not mean *emotionless*, and it certainly doesn't mean less human."

He thought of his own son, Dmitri, and his disabilities, and how people misread him every day. Evander had seen inside Dmitri's mind. He'd experienced the boy's thoughts, the love he had for his mother, the joy he felt whenever Natasha asked him to play.

"The clones want the freedom to choose how to spend their time . . . what to do with their lives. This freedom is an inalienable right that we must grant them."

At this point, his entire body emitted calm. He was glowing, euphoric.

"Freedom of choice for everyone!" a man cried, and

others joined him. "Freedom for humans, freedom for clones, freedom for all!"

Evander chuckled. "Yes, that's right." He paused while the crowd cheered.

"I am no longer your president, as you all know, but I am determined to usher humans and clones peacefully into the future. That work begins here. It begins now—with you."

Some cheers drizzled in before becoming a shower of clapping hands.

He bowed his head, and as he waited for the applause to subside, a harsh whooshing sound coursed through his mind. That strange train that had approached with intense speed during the meeting with Drew once again penetrated his brain, growing louder and stronger as each second passed. The searing pain cut him off from the peace he'd immersed himself in, and he responded with a choked exhalation.

"Da—y?" a warped voice appeared, electrical in nature.

The crowd had finished their applause and waited for Evander to take them to the end of his speech. He squinted into the venue and felt the attention of the masses on him like hands that pulled. But he couldn't look up for long. The pain was too much. He doubled over, his chin crashing into the microphone, his body off-balance. The mic toppled out of its holder and became caught in his suit jacket. He groaned and heard the sound of his own distress amplified across the venue.

The crowd responded with a unified *Oh* followed by a swell of silence.

Evander rocked side to side on the stage floor as some kind of static sparked and vibrated within his head, shaking his consciousness. The train in his mind grew in strength and volume, and he grabbed the sides of his skull with clenched hands.

"Da—dy?"

His brain rattled with the strange sound.

"Daddy!"

Natasha?

It was Natasha!

He writhed in pain as he attempted to speak to her internally: *Baby, where are you? Who took you? Tell me where you are!*

19

E vander was eight minutes into his speech as Fran weathered the roughest, most out-of-control protesters in the farthest depths of the lawn. Every few feet he called to Max but his voice failed to rise above the din. In the distance and on the screens, he saw Evander at the podium, speaking, but he caught only the occasional phrase. He'd been kicked; his feet, stomped on; and every part of his body grabbed and collided with by more people than he could count at this point.

Damn it, Max, look over here!

Harried men and women screeched instead of chanted. They were definitely drunk. He'd noticed several of them tipping back flasks and vaping huge clouds, probably of that supercharged THC that revved users up and smelled like pond scum. Some of them slurred their lame chants about clones going home.

Above the racket, Evander's speech rose, comforting and clear: "We sometimes forget how conflicted the past was . . ."

The sudden harsh call of "Vasquez!" stopped him in his tracks. "Do you see . . . he's doing? Tell him to—" The words became lost as Fran checked over his shoulder and saw Leonard parting the nearby crowd with his massive arms and angry, jutting stride.

With his face pulled long with annoyance, Leonard pointed toward Max and appeared to be saying something, though the crowd still drowned out whatever that was. Something about "away."

Get away? Put away?

"What are you doing here?" Fran shouted. "Go cover the stage like you're supposed to."

"Tell your kid to put his gun away."

This time Fran heard clearly.

His gun? Fran couldn't turn around to check. He didn't want to lose sight of Leonard. "You know what? Stop trying to get him in trouble."

"He was *waving* it around."

"He wouldn't do that," Fran said, sustaining a flailing elbow to his ear. He shook his head and puffed out his chest in a vexed way.

Through the speakers above, Evander's words emerged: "We must once again share in an equal way the protection of this great nation."

Leonard kept coming, traveling like a fire over dried grasses, shoving one guy out of the way and literally lifting and moving a girl who blocked his path.

"What the hell are you doing?" Fran tried to back away but only ended up bumping against the people behind him.

The muscles in Leonard's arms bulged out of his short-sleeved shirt as he seemed to have his sights set not on Fran but beyond him.

Fran turned and yelled, "Max, run! Go! Get out—" Before he knew it, Leonard was right there, his fist like a baseball bat aimed at Fran's face. His big, bulky arm swung out and around, and the knuckles connected solidly with the side of

Fran's head. The area surrounding his temple exploded, and he struggled to see. His right side stung as if he'd been hit by a two-by-four. Fran plowed backward into the people nearest him—wobbling, dizzy, trying to shake off the shock and pain so he could see straight. When did his body get so heavy? All of a sudden, those people who'd caught him weren't there anymore, and he couldn't regain his balance. He stumbled around for a few seconds before he found his face in the dirt.

I have to get up, he thought as he staggered to all fours.

The crowd had bumped out around him as much as it could, as if Fran had contracted a deadly disease they didn't want to catch. He rose to his feet, unsteady as he tried to find the horizon. Leonard stood a couple of yards away, bobbing on the balls of his feet, looking eager to land another punch. He came at Fran again, a wild alien flash in his eyes sent chills up Fran's spine.

He wants to kill me.

And then the buzz of a small rocket came from behind and flew past Fran's ear, so close to his head that his eyeballs vibrated in their sockets. *A rocket?* he thought with groggy confusion.

As if hit by a bus, Leonard jolted upward, jumping and going limp at the same time; blood arced like a small fountain out the side of his head before he dropped out of sight.

Screams rose like flames around Fran, and, oddly, all he could think was, *Lisa is going to kill me.*

The crowd attempted to move in every direction, in *any* direction, but there was barely room to breathe let alone move. The moving was slow as molten lava, with a palpable desperation that caused Fran's head to burn with the pressure. The people around him pushed but didn't get anywhere, an occasional limb came up for air, heads bobbed into each other, elbows thrust into his rib cage. Fran bounced from person to person, somehow overpowering his urge to collapse but unable to reclaim agency. His head throbbed, and his consciousness threatened to shut down. He fought to remain upright, but it was like being in a raft upon rough seas. His leaden head lulled this way and that at the crowd's whim.

Worst of all, he'd lost Max.

He began to sink, a cluster of arms in his face like the branches of trees in a hurricane.

"Oh, no you don't!" It was Max's voice in his ear, his hands reaching for him. "Come on, Dad, lean on me. We've got to move!"

Fran wanted to, but his legs buckled underneath him. Max grunted as he draped Fran's heavy arm across his back and did his best to buoy him up, attempting to guide him out, away. But there were just too many people, too much chaos, not enough strength.

The two of them were trapped.

20

All at once the audience mixed and stirred like a boiling cauldron. Evander's calming influence lost its grip, dried up, dissipated. Humans rushed the clones who guarded the perimeter, and the clones easily took them down. One by one, humans were rendered harmless and led out of the turbulent pit. But there were too many people. Not enough clones to handle them. The humans found pieces of wood to swing, rocks to throw.

Evander watched in horror from his position on the floor of the stage, unsure of what to do next. He'd doubled over, taken out the mic, and communicated with his daughter through a mental connection, imploring her to speak. Then he'd succumbed to a feeling of exhaustion. The next he knew, Elsa joined him onstage, her two fingers upon a pulse point and one tapping her ear.

"Got him," she said with the usual confidence. "Uninjured. Moving out."

Suddenly Martin was there as well. They stood Evander on his feet and started to move him, though he resisted as best he could. He needed to finish his speech, but his feet and legs seemed not to be listening to his commands—it was as if Elsa had taken control.

What the hell happened?

The communication with Natasha had cut through his brain and severed his connection to the peace, but an internal interruption had never caused a crowd to go ballistic like this.

"Gunshot in the back of the park," Elsa said. "We need to get you out of here."

"What? No! I can fix this. Let me do what I have to do." He struggled to break free so he could get back to dispensing the calm, but he could hardly move on his own volition let alone settle his mind and tap into the cosmos.

In spite of his protests, his legs continued to walk him to the side of the stage while Martin skillfully thwarted anyone (even other secret service intent on helping) who came within arm's length. The three of them passed through the exit and out of the crowd's sight.

"Where are Fran and Max?" Evander shouted. "*Do not leave without them.*"

Instead of answering the question, Elsa threw him over her shoulder and descended the steps, Martin sticking close by. "I'm sorry but we have to get you out of here, sir."

Elsa possessed the strength of three men. Why didn't he know this? They'd never been in a situation where she found it necessary to manhandle him into submission. But now he knew. She was superhuman. Literally.

At the bottom of the stairs, she set him on his feet. "Your safety takes precedence, I'm afraid."

"Fine," Evander said. "Someone has to find Fran and Max."

"Affirmative." With a tilt of her head, Elsa signaled Martin, who took off like a deer into the crowded lawn. Evander watched as the people parted the same way crowds made way when Jovian royalty passed through. He'd never seen Martin do that before. *Has he always been able to do these things?*

As Evander lingered on the magic of Martin, Elsa guided him down a tunnel they hadn't traveled through on the way in. It ended in the parking lot, the van already waiting.

"Here we are," she said. "Please get in."

"I'm not leaving until Fran and—"

"Your safety takes precedence, sir," she said, and this time he was certain that she somehow had manipulated him into the vehicle without touching him. His arms and legs did what was necessary to climb in against his will. Elsa crawled in after him, acting like the stopper of an empty bottle, making sure he stayed inside. Once they were seated, the sliding door closed.

As Evander strained to see out the window, he felt her release him and he could once again move at will.

Elsa gazed upward. "Martin's on it," she told him before easing into a meditative state of silence.

Evander sank into the seat. *What just happened?* he asked himself for a second time. First, he'd heard his daughter but couldn't place where she was, or with whom. Uncle Jimmy, maybe? He had to believe whoever had taken her encouraged her to reach him through the oneness, though she'd never used it before. Next, he had not fixed the problem between the humans and clones, and may have even made it worse. And third, he'd lost Fran and Max, and doubted Martin would singlehandedly pluck them out from the panicked crowd of thousands—as magical as he might be.

Elsa tapped her ear and said, "Martin has them."

The van's door opened like a great metal mouth, and Fran materialized, stumbling inside as if lifted by an invisible force. He dropped onto the seat in front of Evander, knees and face first. In a loose fetal position, his shoulders rose and fell in heaves. Elsa tended to him, readjusting his position so he sat properly, with his ass in the chair and his head above it, his upper body propped against the side of the seat. Then Elsa reached into one of the van's compartments for what appeared to be an ice pack and placed it upon a sprawling red-and-purple splotch on the side of his face, near his temple.

This made Fran groan like a bear.

Max, with his security squad shirt ripped and hanging from one shoulder, climbed in next. "Dad, Dad, are you okay?" He struggled out of the shirt and let it drop to the floor.

"I'm fine, just let me . . . " Fran's words slid out the side of his mouth.

He seemed anything but fine.

Martin entered the van looking crisp and clean, not a wrinkle or smudge on his black suit. Evander had always known he was good, loyal, and efficient, but this? Beyond amazing.

Martin took his place beside Evander, and Max stared with wonder. "How did you find us—how did you get us out? I thought we were dead for sure."

Elsa tapped her ear and said, "Go." The van took off like a rocket on wheels. Then she reached into one of the interior's many compartments and pulled out a white T-shirt and handed it to Max.

"What happened out there?" she said as he put it on.

"Leonard made us cover the crowd, and then he tried to kill my father." Max pulled the shirt over his torso.

Fran grumbled something about being fine.

"Leonard turned into a frickin' monster." Max appeared to replay the scene in his mind, his mouth twisting in horror. "I was scared to death. He just kept coming. He wasn't going to stop—I had to do it. He tried to kill my dad!"

Fran squinted in Max's direction. "Wait a minute," he said, his lids only half open. "That was your gun that went off? *You* shot Len—"

"I'm sorry, I'm sorry," Max said, chin trembling. "I had to."

"I told you under *no circumstance*—" Fran grabbed his forehead and exhaled a groan. "You almost shot *me*," he muttered before collapsing, his head dashing against the window.

Elsa reached across the aisle and stabbed Fran's leg with some kind of injection.

Max looked ready to lunge. "What did you just give him?"

"It's okay," Evander said, conjuring the calm. "Elsa is trained medically."

"Is Leonard dead?" Elsa said to no one in particular.

"Injured. First degree. Head wound." Martin replied. "Fifty percent chance of survival."

Evander reached out and placed his hand on Max's shoulder. "Leonard works for Starbright. He'll be in good hands."

"As soon as the gun went off, everyone in that crowd went crazy," Max said. "That's *my* fault."

"The clones will get it under control," Evander told him. "It will be all right."

Max sniffed before releasing a stifled sob. "I knew something was wrong with Leonard. I knew it when he hit me the other day—"

"Hit you?" Evander said.

Max whimpered a little, his shoulders rising toward his ears. "I complained about work, and I know that was wrong, but he hit me without warning. He dropped me right there in the break room."

No one at Starbright had ever broken the code of nonviolence. Clones weren't violent by nature, and it was near impossible to provoke them.

"Then Caroline promoted him to co-captain," Max muttered.

"Promoted him?" *What was she up to?*

Evander looked to Elsa. "Who called the security squad to this event? Why were Leonard and the others even there?" Caroline had ignored the occurrences in Philadelphia since the beginning. Suddenly she decided to send security? That didn't make sense.

"I was not informed of their presence prior to our arrival," Elsa said. "Martin?"

Martin's eyes rolled back and twitched back and forth as if scrolling data. "No, ma'am. I have no information of that nature."

Normally secret service would be informed of all security squad members on the premises.

Evander searched his mind for any sign of Caroline or David and the Jovian oneness, but found none. Then, in as much detail as he could imagine, he replayed Natasha's attempt to break through. He reached into the vast expanse that was his mind. Where once he faced chatter, he now found emptiness, a sprawling desert of nothing.

It had finally happened. He was completely cut off.

"Natasha!" he called internally, the desperation in his voice vaulting through space unhindered. "Natasha!"

There was no answer.

For the first time in his life, Evander felt utterly alone.

21

Fran's face throbbed from temple to jaw. But he was alive, and Max was there, safe beside him in the van.

What's next? Where are we going? What does Evander need?

He tried to speak but only managed a grumble.

"I'm here, Dad. You're fine. Don't worry."

"But I—" His head hurt like a fierce hangover—like he drank something awful and then whacked himself in the head with the bottle when it was empty.

"Elsa says you've got a concussion. They'll fix you up, though, don't worry."

The van sped down the highway, rising and falling with the dips in the road as the hum of the wheels made white noise in his ears.

From what Fran could see, Evander murmured into his cell, Elsa took inventory of one of the van's many storage compartments, and Martin appeared to be in some kind of a meditative trance: hands on lap, body in full alignment, attention internally focused.

They had almost died out there. The kid had shot

Leonard. Fran had never been so upset and proud of Max at the same time. Max shouldn't have done it. Shouldn't have fired his weapon. But then, when the crowd threatened to swallow them whole, the kid who wore a robe and hid in his room had come through. Taken charge. Literally took hold of Fran and kept him afloat long enough for the rescue to come.

How is that even possible? Maybe this job actually is good for him.

Except that Max had started a battle with that one gunshot.

The pain in Fran's head would not be ignored—the throbbing began at the height of his temple and crashed into the roots of his teeth. No doubt clips of the incident were being broadcast across the nation. The entire population of humans, clones, hybrids, and Jovians might be seeing closeups of Max's face right now.

Oh my God, Lisa is going to kill me.

"My phone," he shouted. "I need my phone."

"Dad, calm down. It's missing. Leonard probably knocked it out of your pocket with that nasty right hook."

Fran preferred not to hear those words spoken in front of Evander, or anyone else. "Give me yours. Have you called your mother?"

Max pressed his lips together as if his patience wore thin. "I texted her. She's fine."

"This isn't something you type about, Max! Give me your phone right now."

Max handed it over with a huff, muttering, "She's much calmer than you are right now."

Evander glanced their way, still murmuring into his phone, probably talking to his wife the same way Fran should have been talking to his.

Fran lowered his voice: "Has Mom seen the video clips? Have they made it out there yet? What did she say?"

"Footage of the incident has reached the airwaves," Elsa said through her usual calm, "but nothing about you or Max yet. It's under control."

"Mom knows we're fine because I told her we are. Don't say something that makes her switch on the news."

"She's at work, at the hospital. There's no chance the news isn't on. She could be seeing your face on camera right now. And I told you *under no circumstances* were you to draw your—"

"Ugh!" Max folded his skinny body over his lap and pulled at his hair, his kinky curls standing tall. "He was going to *kill* you!" he said.

With his cell pressed to his ear, Evander shut them both up with raised brows in their direction.

"Sorry," Fran said. He sat back and breathed in. "You did the right thing. I just wish—"

"I hadn't been the one to start the war?" Max asked. "Yeah, me too."

"It's not a war, and it's gonna be all right," Fran said, though he doubted "all right" was possible. The video footage would be out there sooner rather than later. And then Max would be known throughout the country—throughout the world—as the guy who'd fired the shot. The kid who'd started the battle between humans and clones.

And then what on earth would the Vasquez family do?

Go into hiding? Become recluses in the woods somewhere. No small town in Russia would be able to conceal them the way it had hidden Svetlana and baby Evander from the Jovians. So what would the answer be? Put their robes on and slam their bedroom doors? Or move into Starbright and live with the Jovians?

If he didn't feel so damn dire just then, he might have

153

laughed at that idea. God knows he didn't want to live with the Jovians. Working with them was more than enough.

As he gazed out the window, his brainstorming ventured one step further: they could climb aboard a spaceship like Svetlana had and rocket into another universe.

At that, his body vibrated with the frisson of knowing. Like electricity riding over his skin, the hairs on his arms leapt up and took notice. He let it pass like a chill in the air.

"Where we headed?" he asked, noticing all at once how difficult it was to hold up his aching head.

"Starbright," Elsa said without glancing in his direction.

"We just told you that three seconds ago," Max said. He looked to Elsa. "Are you sure he's gonna be okay?"

22

The van careened past the security hut, a guard waving them in. For a moment Evander expected Jovian security to stop the van, but of course they were letting him in. He was Evander Peterman, Jovian royalty, former three-term president. His presence intimidated none of the Jovian elite. They'd cut him off from the oneness so he no longer knew their plans. Whether he lived on Earth or Io, Caroline had already managed to push him out of the inner circle and possibly had his daughter kidnapped to distract him.

He wondered.

Would she? And if so, why?

The doors of the van slid open as they glided up to the main entrance. Evander ordered Martin to take Fran and Max to the infirmary. Martin looked to Elsa for her nonverbal acquiescence before agreeing to do so.

Evander entered the building, determined to get answers as he climbed the spiral staircase to the balcony that led to the family wing. He entered Caroline's empty office. The room exuded a sterile, emotionless feel that matched her personality. Clean, smooth, and cool, her desk stood in front of a three-tiered bookshelf, all of the furnishings a well-shined mahogany, empty save for a stack of atlases, a few primitive sculptures, a vase here and there, and globes of Earth and Jupiter. In a back corner of the room, casually placed upon the file cabinet, another two globes stared at him like a pair of eyes. It was Io and Europa, Jupiter's icy moons. Those were new.

"Let's check the lab," he told Elsa.

They continued down the corridor and entered the laboratory, potent in scent, vinegar and isopropyl alcohol, some sort of lemony soap mixed in. He could be wrong. His olfactory senses had never been his best.

"There's a microscope with a slide in the back station," Elsa said, though she remained at the front entrance. Her AI vision never missed a thing.

He went to it and looked through the eyepiece. "Blood cells," he said out loud. "DNA." A folder rested beside the microscope. He opened it. Only one piece of paper lay inside. "Dmitri Jovian" was written in pencil followed by some numbers and what appeared to be scientific code. The words "Muscular atrophy" as well.

"Dmitri?" he said. "Why is she studying Dmitri's lab work?" The DNA tests had been done as soon as Dmitri was born. Same for Natasha. Why revisit it now?

"I don't know, sir," Elsa said. "They're in the conference room."

"Who, specifically?"

"Royalty. Caroline, Constance, David, Leo, Miran—"

"Thank you," he said, closing the file. At the end of the corridor, he found the door to the conference room open. Caroline occupied the head of the table, as usual, and gave no indication of being happy or unhappy to see him. Miranda sat opposite her, in his place. *Interesting.* Leo,

David, and Aunt Constance took the chairs in the middle. One uniformed clone stood guard at each of the room's corners.

"Greetings, all," Evander said as he strode in. "I guess I missed the memo pertaining to this meeting."

"Oh, look who it is," Miranda said. "Back from the war, and without a scratch. I suppose you can thank Jovian technology for that."

He raised his brows in question.

"You can thank Constance for your hybrids and their AI enhancements. It's the wave of the future, as they say."

Elsa remained posted at the entry door, no sign of offense, or distress, on her face.

Evander passed Miranda a baffled look.

"Go ahead, Evander," she said. "Thank her. You're human, you know how to do that."

"If I owe Constance my gratitude, then certainly, I thank her." He bowed his head in the direction of his aunt, who, like an innocent old grandmother, pursed her lips and gave a humble nod.

Evander approached the empty chair beside David and grasped the top of it. "So, what's on the agenda?"

"Well, you made a mess of Philadelphia, as we predicted you would," Miranda said with a dramatic sigh.

Caroline's serious demeanor remained steadfast. Did she approve of the way Miranda spoke to him? If it bothered her, she gave no sign of it.

He stood unmoving in front of them, knowing all at once what it felt like to be an unpopular member of the family. Knowing what it felt like to be Svetlana, it occurred to him with a pang of sadness. Caroline had never liked the fact that the Jovians needed Svetlana and therefore had to deal with her, accommodate her. Maybe he shouldn't have convinced her to leave.

Then again, leaving meant getting away from *them* and landing in a place where she could be happy.

He stood straighter. He should at least appear in control, even if that wasn't how he felt. "I'd like a word with my grandmother, if you all wouldn't mind. It's important."

No one moved. David's hands rested flat on the table in front of him, his eyes remained closed but active, the skin around them wrinkled and ashen like an old man's. Miranda made a very human expression of annoyance. Leo turned his head almost imperceptibly in Caroline's direction. Constance, with her arms straight at her sides, stared out the window.

"I told you there was nothing you could do," Caroline said, "that you must let evolution take its course."

"Yes, I know. Can we talk, just you and me?" he said nicely, playing the concerned grandson.

"If you had left it alone, President Abela would not be dealing with a battle in Philadelphia right now."

"In all fairness, she asked me to speak. I was there because she requested my help. And it's not a battle. The clones are handling it in their usual manner."

Caroline clasped her hands and placed them in her lap. He had the distinct feeling that she was merely tolerating him. "You could have refused," she said. "And you should have. I asked you to go to Io, where your grandfather needs you right now, and you chose not to. And now there's a battle, and not only are humans dying but the divide between human and clone has expanded exponentially."

He knew about the casualties. Three, from what he'd been told. A heart attack, a broken neck from a slip off one of the container barricades, and someone who'd fallen on a wooden stake she'd attempted to wield like a sword. "There have been some accidents—"

"And bound to be a lot more," Caroline said without

remorse. "One thing humans are good at is getting themselves killed."

Evander sank back like a reprimanded child. *What kind of protector am I?*

"I'm sorry," he said. "With my daughter missing, perhaps my judgment isn't at its best."

"That's an understatement," Miranda muttered.

Caroline raised her chin, a gesture that caused Miranda to stand and walk out. Leo and Constance followed. David remained seated, eyes bouncing with abandon under his dark lids.

Evander lowered into the chair beside Caroline and said, "You're not happy with me."

"It's not a matter of happy or unhappy. You made a bad decision. It's human nature to do so."

That, he knew, was meant to be a slap in the face. He couldn't help but sense her disdain when she spoke of his human side. The side that was Svetlana. The woman she couldn't tame. The one she'd sent out of this universe—and he'd helped her do it.

"Where is Natasha, do you know? Or does David? I heard her voice today, in my mind, but—"

"I know no more than you. David has been working tirelessly to mend communications, as you can see." She lifted a hand in his direction.

As far as Evander could tell, David's body occupied the chair, but his mind took him far away. "What could be causing the trouble?" he asked.

"We don't know. I've already told you that." Her stare chilled him as much as Miranda's cold words had.

This was not the way he'd wanted this talk to go. He reached out and grasped Caroline's hand, which was smooth and dense, not unlike marble.

"Please listen to me and keep an open mind when you consider what I say."

"I always do," she said, her demeanor unwavering.

"Drew came to me."

Her eyelids twitched.

"You know that he and some other clones are leading the protest."

Her nonresponse indicated that she did. It had to hurt. Drew had been her highest-ranking clone. She'd trusted him. Which was humorous considering she no longer trusted Evander. Why was that? Because they disagreed? Or because he was the child of Svetlana?

"He wants a promise for his people," he said.

"I will make no such promise."

"Then the clones won't protect you, they won't protect Earth."

"They will."

She spoke with formidable strength, the kind that slammed directly into his chest, but he couldn't accept it. He had to keep trying.

"I'm telling you that I've spoken to Drew," he said, "and his people are not going to back down. You say I must trust you, but you also must trust me. Especially when it comes to knowing clones like Drew. I have a talent for reading them. And I can tell you without any doubt that he's set on this."

She remained steadfast in her stillness.

"Caroline," he said through an exasperated breath, "you say that an intergalactic threat is imminent. An uncivilized entity may be traveling to Earth. We're going to need the clones to defend the planet. I can set up a meeting with Drew. You can negotiate with him. He wants to speak with you."

"The clones *will* defend Earth," she said.

Evander interlaced his fingers and placed his hands on

the table with a frustrated thump. "Okay," he said, shaking his head. "How will you convince them?"

"Leave that to me."

"All you have to do is promise fairness, an opportunity for a free life," he said, his words swift and desperate. "What they're asking for isn't unreasonable. They're a devoted species. Many of them will still choose to pursue a life of security and defense, but you have to—"

"I don't have to do anything," she said, sharply. "Let alone make promises."

The words crashed through Evander's brain. He didn't just hear them, he felt them. They rang like electricity inside his head and rode over any remaining determination to win this argument by wrestling it to its knees. Caroline had never treated him with such disdain. She once thought the world of him. Or so that was how it had seemed.

"Please, Grandmother, at least meet with Drew. I'm sorry if I've offended you."

She looked down at the table, and he thought perhaps she regretted her defiance and would consider his plea, but he couldn't hear her thoughts. He didn't have any idea what she was thinking. Then she turned her head in David's direction. Evander did the same and noticed David's closed eyes resting peacefully, unmoving.

"If you want to make it up to me," Caroline said, "you'll go to Io."

23

F ran and Max entered the small infirmary. Straight ahead stood an examination table, a sheet of paper pulled across its top. To the side, two chairs backed against the wall. A small desk with a sleek square of a tablet on top tucked into the back corner. Fran did a double-take when he first saw an Andrew clone wearing white lab attire manning the desk. He looked to be about thirty-five. Unlike the occasional Andrew clone Fran had met in the past, this one approached, wanting to shake his hand.

"I'm Andy," he said, already studying the injury throbbing upon the right side of Fran's face. "That looks like it hurts. What happened?"

The Andrew clones boggled Fran's mind on a good day, tempting him to give in to feelings of familiarity. But this wasn't Andrew, and even though Fran felt as if someone had stuffed a pillow into his skull, and every blink of his lids had the same effect as someone pressing their thumb into the fresh bruise covering his temple, he realized he didn't know this guy.

"Got into a scuffle." Each syllable he spoke thumped his brain. "Nothing major."

Max, in one of the chairs, paused his scrolling or texting, or whatever he was doing, to scoff. He was annoyed that Fran had made him enter the examination room with him—he'd made that clear—but Fran couldn't exactly leave the kid alone in the corridor with this place crawling with clones who, by now, may have learned what had happened to Leonard. Not that they would retaliate, necessarily. He hoped.

It would have been nice if Martin had stuck around, but he literally walked them to the infirmary and left them to fend for themselves. Clones didn't usually seek revenge, but after what Fran had seen in the last week, he couldn't be sure they wouldn't.

Andy patted the examination table. "Have a seat," he said.

Fran removed his security belt and various gear, placing it on the empty chair beside Max.

"This is your son?" Andy asked without taking his focus off the wound.

"Yeah," Fran answered with reluctance, not in the mood for sharing.

"Obviously. He looks just like you."

People usually said Max looked like Lisa, so this made Fran take pause. He supposed the kid more and more resembled him, and there was something satisfying about that and also something telling: Max was finally growing up.

"Thank you," Fran said.

Max frowned at him, as if to say, "You're happy about that?"

Andy shined a light into Fran's eyes, squinting as he gazed into them. The Andrew clone's eyes were the toughest part to handle. That blue-green color, unlike anyone else's, and yet duplicated who knows how many times in the form of

Andrew clones. Evander had the same hue; Fran couldn't forget that.

Seeing Andy made him wish he could have a beer with his old buddy. Andrew was so normal. So easygoing. Sometimes Fran imagined a conversation they might have if they ever had a chance to talk again. They would bitch and moan about the state of the country and the world, and maybe even laugh (and cry) about what Fran learned about Jovians and the universe the past twenty or so years. Andrew would pull a face and say something like, "You know my family. They're weird."

Then again, it would be a pretty serious conversation overall. Who would have thought either of them would end up the way they had?

Andy touched the area beside Fran's temple. "Whoever got you, got you good. If they'd hit the temple full on, it would have been lights out. Did you lose consciousness at any point?"

"Yes, he did," Max said. "About twenty minutes, half an hour."

Fran turned to get a clear view of Max's face. "Are you joking? I mean, I remember shutting my eyes, but—"

"He was completely out of it," Max said. "Elsa gave him something so he wouldn't end up in a coma."

Fran didn't remember any of this, and Max better not have been making it up.

"She shot you in the leg with something," Max said, with the utmost seriousness. "You actually shrieked."

Fran's face warmed. "And you let her?"

Max shrugged. "Evander was right there, so I figured—"

"Oh, right." Fran wished thinking didn't hurt so much.

Andy put a hand on his shoulder. "She did the right thing. Now, lie back, remain still, and we'll have you out of here in no time."

Fran lay back, his injured head like a medicine ball. He watched Andy return to his computer. *So this is what Andrew would have been like as a doctor.*

"Look at the ceiling," Andy said.

Fran stared up. A white metal panel parted, and a silver globe the size of a billiard ball lowered on a thin, taut wire. Its many parts twisted this way and that like the slivers of a puzzle trying to find the just-right combination. It came closer, cautious as a bird, hovering and buzzing, its parts gently clicking. Something snapped into place, and it flew back up, disappearing into the opening in the white metal panel, which then closed.

Andy typed a few keys on the computer and studied the screen. "Oh, yes, there it is. That's pretty severe. . . . Uh, okay, let me just check the . . . oh, good, good. We can fix that." And then he said, "Hold still, please," and pressed another key.

"Wait—should I leave?" Max's voice went up an octave.

He couldn't stand the sight of blood, which sometimes caused dizziness to the point of passing out.

"You can leave if you want to," Andy said in a preoccupied manner, "but this won't take long."

Fran raised one arm toward Max, his hand clenched in a fist. "No, you can't," he enunciated, each utterance stabbing his wound. "I need you where I can see you."

"Okay, but I really don't want to—"

"Just look away, Max," Fran said through gritted teeth.

Fran wasn't worried about what Andy would do next. He would never forget the time he and Svetlana broke into Starbright with the intention of finding the spaceship. One second Leo stood on the balcony, and the next, he'd somehow rendered Fran unconscious. Fran woke in the lab, by himself, scared out of his wits. He'd thought they'd wanted to study him—or experiment, God forbid. But then David arrived and told him they could replace the arm he'd lost to a bullet wound four years prior, and did he want them to do that?

He'd trusted David that day and trusted Andy now. Having access to Jovian medical technology was a wonderful thing.

He gazed at the ceiling, watching as the panel parted once again and the silver globe reappeared like a bird through a vent. It didn't touch him, but he felt something on the right side of his face shift at the skin level and then flatten deeper within. Like cloth under a hot iron, the swollen tissue decompressed, smoothing bit by bit.

The throbbing faded. And then the light no longer made him squint in pain, and his thoughts flowed without effort.

The little globe backed up a couple of inches, pausing before orbiting his head and returning the way it had come.

He hadn't realized how badly his face hurt until the pain receded.

"Very good," Andy said, staring at the computer screen. "Your file says you're a fast healer." He looked up at Max. "You're lucky to have his genes."

Max gave a half-assed nod, as if he wasn't too sure about that.

Andy walked up to Fran once more. "You can sit up now. Give it a test drive."

Fran pushed up to his elbows.

Andy's arm curved around his back and bolstered him up as he came to a seated position.

He studied Fran closely. "Your face has returned to normal size. How does it feel?"

"*Normal* size?" Fran chuckled as he reveled in the lack of pain. He tilted his head this way and that, then pressed the area around his temple with caution. "It's like it never happened."

Andy grinned. "Great, then you're all set." He stepped back to his computer. "Try not to get into any more fights."

That was something Andrew would have said. Fran hopped down from the table and picked up his belt, fixing it around his waist. "Can I ask you something," he said, "and I hope you won't be offended."

"Sure."

"You're a clone, so how did you become a doctor? Why aren't you working some kind of security, like the others?"

"That's a good question." He came around the front of his desk and leaned back into it, crossing one leg over the other. "When I was a new clone, I showed a special interest and aptitude for Jovian medicine and healing methods. Caroline recognized that and appointed me to the job."

"Caroline?"

"You seem surprised."

"From what I've seen, she appoints 99 percent of clones to security."

"That's true. And we're all trained in defense, regardless."

"Oh?" Fran's ears perked.

"First and foremost," he said in a singsong fashion.

"I didn't know—"

A commotion in the corridor erupted. The sound of metal bars adjusting and rattling, footsteps nearing. "This way!" someone called.

"Excuse me a second." Andy passed in front of Fran and opened the infirmary door, then said, "You're free to go, Mr. Vasquez. Careful, now. Emergency coming through."

Fran stepped toward the door and peered down the hall. Four of the security squad, their gloves and uniforms blood spattered, guided a stretcher toward them. *Was it Leonard?* In his hazy thinking, Fran had assumed Leonard would have been rushed to the nearest hospital. But the Jovians cared for their own, of course.

"Max, let's go," Fran said with renewed urgency. "Hurry."

Max hopped to, and the two of them fast-walked out of the room with their heads down. What they saw close up would no doubt be branded in Max's memory forever: Leonard's bulky body turned on its side, unnaturally twisted and dead looking. His face concealed by an oxygen mask, everything red with blood. Fran would not have been able to identify him had he not known what happened on Independence Lawn a couple of hours before.

The kid rushed ahead.

"The stairs," Fran said as calmly as possible.

Max glanced back, over his shoulder. "That wasn't him, was it?"

"I don't know. Just keep going."

"Oh my God, it was him . . . I knew it. He's going to die!"

"The Jovians won't let that happen."

"He looked pretty dead to me."

"Just keep walking."

Max walked backward. "Where to?"

Fran mouthed the words *parking lot*.

They raced into the red room and out the back exit, picking up the pace as they descended the outdoor staircase and ran in the direction of Fran's parking space. The fact that they'd made it outside without being stopped poured adrenaline into Fran's veins. The little bit of daylight that remained surprised him—it felt like it should be midnight—it had to be 8 p.m. or maybe later. No one was pulling into the lot or backing out.

"You think he's still alive?" Max said, brows wobbling as if he were on the verge of losing it.

"Martin said he has a fifty-fifty chance," Fran reminded him, "but I'm sure it's better than that. Remember what they did for my arm?"

"So they can save him? Even if he's dead, they can bring him back?"

"First of all, we don't know that he's dead."

"If they don't bring him back," Max said, spiraling into panic, "I will have started a war *and* killed someone. They have to bring him back."

"Take it easy, Max. You were protecting me. Never forget that."

The car locks thunked and doors popped open. Max jumped in, and Fran did the same. He pressed the start button, the dashboard emitting the usual light blue glow. He backed up, then put it in drive and floored it out of there, back tires fishtailing.

Beside him, Max slumped in mental pain, his face tense with clenched teeth. Fran had seen this type of thing happen to young recruits working for the FBI. Whatever denial had initially protected Max from feeling the reality of what had played out was gone. He'd been preoccupied with the fact that Fran was injured, but now that Fran sat beside him good as new, Max remembered what he'd done to keep him alive. He needed a rope to grab onto or risked submerging in a whirlpool of regret and fear.

"Hey, Max," Fran said, "call your mom. Tell her the Jovians healed my injuries. Tell her we're on our way."

"Yeah. Okay. I was texting her before. I told her most of it."

"Well, now you can give her the good news that we're coming home, you know, and just hear her voice."

Max pulled the cell from his pocket, pressed a button, then another. When he said, "Mom, it's me," his voice quivered and he took a sharp inhale. There was no way to keep a lid on strong emotions when talking to your mom after a horrible ordeal.

In the kitchen, the three of them stood by the island, swaying in a three-person hug. Fran pressed his cheek to Lisa's and reveled in the comfort of her presence. Silence dropped in like the calm after the storm, and he couldn't help thinking, *Now what do we do?*

When they pulled apart, Max said, "Are we going to be okay?"

The muscles in Fran's face stiffened as he tried to look sincere. He'd never been a good liar. "Yeah. I'll try to reach Evander in a little bit."

"What about your job?" Max's frightened voice raised Fran's disposition to protect him.

"I'm not worrying about that right now and neither should you. Evander's on our side. We'll be fine no matter what." Fran pointed to the fridge. "Get me a bottle of water, and one for yourself. I'm sure you're dehydrated."

Max went to the fridge, and Lisa took Fran's hand. She had that tired, "I just worked a double shift" look, her face swollen with fatigue. "I thought long, anxious days like these were over when you left the FBI. I never imagined I'd have to worry about a war breaking out in Pennsylvania—or Starbright security being part of it."

"I know," he told her, "I'm sorry."

Max handed him the water.

Lisa reached out and placed her hand on Max's shoulder, forcing him to face her. "Are you okay, sweetie?" She took his cheeks in her hands and gazed into his eyes.

"I thought I was," he said, "but now that I'm home—"

"Hey," she said, her voice low and serious, "you saved your father. You did the right thing."

He fought his quivering chin as he stepped out of Lisa's reach. "I just wanna go to my room."

"Good idea. You must be exhausted. We'll figure out a plan. Don't worry about anything."

"I'll try," he said, slouching his way down the hall.

"He needs a few minutes to himself," Fran said under his breath.

"I'm sure. Some therapy too, no doubt."

Fran said "uh-huh," gazing at the floor. "Have you been watching the news and checking headlines?"

"I have. Nothing so far about Max or you."

"Evander's people are trying to control the airwaves, but I don't know. This whole thing is so big. There's no way someone didn't get it on video."

"They're Jovian. I'm sure they can handle it."

"Yeah, let's hope." He gulped the water.

"I still think we should get out of here," Lisa said. "Just for a few days. Find someplace quiet to hunker down until we see how it pans out. I mean, have you even spoken to Leo? How are you going to be able to go back to work?"

"I haven't thought ahead that far. And I agree we should leave town, but where to? If video footage gets out, it'll be nationwide."

She closed her eyes and smoothed her fingers across her brow. "I'm so damn tired. I can't think. I'm off three twelve-hour days, and you know how that leaves me. I'm surprised I don't have a migraine right now."

He reached for her and pulled her into a hug, so damn grateful to have her in his life. "I'm really sorry about this."

"God knows it's not your fault. Let's just sleep for a few hours, maybe get up around three and see where we're at. We can't be home if this thing breaks wide open, but I'm useless right now. I'm drained from worrying all day." She touched the area where Fran's injury occurred. "It's barely a stain, but I'll bet this was pretty ugly before the Jovians worked their magic."

"Oh, yeah, I'm good as new. Again."

A puff of relief passed over her lips. "My six-million dollar man."

"Ha ha," he said, giving her a squeeze. "We'll hit the road. Maybe find a place to camp? We have plenty of gear. That way, we can keep to ourselves."

"I've already packed a bunch of stuff in duffle bags. They're in the front hall."

"I figured you'd be prepared."

She smiled the kind of smile that could almost make him believe everything would be all right. "I'm a mother," she said. "That's what we do."

24

That night, the van sped into the Peterman driveway, and Elsa led Evander to his front door, scanning the grounds as they went. Martin headed for the backyard. Several other secret service patrolled nearby. For the first time ever, Evander wondered where Elsa's home was. Maybe she and Martin lived together. Roommates or . . . more possibly? He laughed at himself: now he was really thinking like a human.

Before Evander stepped inside, he said, "You need to go home and get some rest."

"That's not my thing, sir."

"You don't rest?" And then he realized he already knew the answer. "Of course you don't."

"Similar to the way you don't."

It was true that Jovians rarely slept. But he wasn't 100 percent Jovian, and he did need to recharge from time to time. "But you've always gone home in the past, haven't you?" he asked.

"No. And neither has Martin. We're never far from you. Even when you think we've gone."

That was a little creepy.

"What do you do, just back into a corner somewhere and count down the hours like a grandfather clock?"

"Ha. That's funny, sir. And no, we're always on high alert. Your safety takes precedence."

"Okay," he said. "Well, I guess that's great. Thank you for your service."

"I love my job, sir. And so does Martin. Good night."

He stepped into the foyer, dimly lit by a lamp on top of the console that also held a basket for keys and loose change, not that he ever had either of those things. Some light spilled onto the wood floor from the kitchen. He followed it into the garden room, where he found Nadia on the couch by herself, hugging a pillow to her chest while Dmitri lay draped over the coffee table as he often did. Her face was drawn and pale. She seemed beaten, her spirits low.

"Nadia. I'm so sorry. You didn't have to wait up."

"With all that is going on, there is no way I can sleep." Her Russian accent became more pronounced when she was tired. "I saw what happened. I saw your speech and how you collapsed on the stage. I saw the battle. And then Elsa sent a message, and I knew you were safe."

"Yes," he said, waiting for what she would say next.

"But my daughter is still missing," she said through the preoccupied aura of a person numbed by worry, "so when I saw people attacking clones and clones wrestling them to the ground, I didn't care."

She looked up at him, and her pain and fear and sense of abandonment seeped into his skin and made him want to hold her and apologize and promise that everything would be all right.

"Right now," she continued, "all I can think about is Natasha and how no one can find her." She paused to swallow her pain, frowning with her whole face—her blame, like the tip of a knife poking the center of his chest. Then she said it: "Not even you."

Dmitri made a "Na, Na, Na" sound, his nickname for Natasha.

Evander bent forward and touched his son's arm. "Don't worry, we'll find her," he said, and the boy wrenched back from his touch, as he always did. Evander sat beside Nadia on the couch and pulled her close, holding her trembling body as she fought the sadness that threatened to overtake her.

"She's alive," he said. "She reached out to me today. At the protest. While I was on stage."

"Natasha did?" Nadia said, drawing back from their embrace. "So, it's happened."

He answered with a reluctant nod. "I believe so."

"She is part of the oneness?"

It was clearly an accusation.

"Wherever she is," he said, "she tried to use it—or some other method of telepathy. I'm not sure. Communications are down at this point. At least for me. It's a vast empty plain, and I can't tell you how odd that is." He closed his eyes and sank into the kind of despair that threatened to sweep him away. "The oneness isn't there, but Natasha tried to reach me. Her voice was distorted and distant—and powerful—like it had broken through a barrier."

"But it was her, you're sure?" Nadia balanced the tips of her quivering fingers on her lips as if unsure of whether to be excited or disappointed.

"It was her. Yes."

"What did she say?"

"Just *Daddy*, but I heard her and sensed her presence as if she were right there, beside me. And if the oneness comes back, I'll reach out to her. She can tell me where she is, and I'll find her. This nightmare will be over."

"Our daughter was taken, and the oneness disappeared," Nadia said. "That can't be a coincidence."

"No, I don't think it is."

"That means one of your family members is responsible. They unplugged the communications so no one would know. But why? Why do they want Natasha?"

"Caroline and David don't know anything," he said, but even as he spoke the words aloud, he doubted their validity. He felt himself shrugging and, mindful of it, willed himself to stop. "I can't see into the oneness, so I don't know. There's so much going on. So much that I can't get a grip on—" He stopped. There was no use for this sort of complaining.

Nadia sat back and studied him. "I've never seen you like this. It isn't like you not to know."

A bolt of shame flashed over him. His whole life he'd handled problems large and small, found solutions, made the necessary connections and communications—and now, when it mattered most to his wife and children, he suffered a powerlessness he didn't know how to overcome. Nadia's disappointment wound around him like an overly tight tie around his neck.

"I don't like it either," he said. "But Natasha reached me. That's one good thing."

He didn't mention that he assumed she was very far away or that she might be with Uncle Jimmy—he had no proof that Jimmy had taken her. But thinking Jimmy may have taken her comforted him, while thinking someone else may have taken her did not.

Hope welled in Nadia's eyes. "Well, where can she be? I can't understand why she would wander away from us in the first place. And if she didn't wander away, how is it possible that no one saw who took her? I just need to know she's okay."

Evander had failed for the third time that day. He couldn't

reassure his wife that Natasha was okay because he didn't know if she was. She was alive. That was all he knew.

He took Nadia's hand like a bird in his palm. Dmitri remained quiet but not sleeping, his keys chiming every now and again.

"You know, this whole thing has made me realize," Nadia said, "that I don't want to do this anymore."

"We'll get her back. I promise, I'll—"

"I believe we *will* get her back. I have to believe that. But that's not what I mean. I can't live like this anymore, Evander." She gazed into his eyes, pleading with him. "I worry about my children every day. They are the most precious things in my life, and I am tired of living in fear. I want to be the kind of mother who can go out with her children when she pleases, take them to the park without a three-ring circus following after. We are isolated for reasons of safety, I understand, and yet, look what's happened. Even with all the trouble we go through, Natasha has been taken."

She was right. He'd failed to protect them.

"When she comes home," she said, "I need to make some changes."

He startled internally, as if waking from a bad dream. "What do you mean?"

"I agreed to marry you, to enter this life with you, because I loved you as soon as I met you, and I still do. I always will." Her eyes met his with the bittersweetness of both love and pain. "I didn't marry you because you would be president one day. I did not want the fame. Watching you succeed was exciting for many years. And I was proud to do so much good for mistreated children and animals tortured in labs. These things mean the world to me. But the rest of it, being part of this Jovian family? It's too much. They are too powerful. I cannot accept it anymore. I think Svetlana had the right idea when you were a child and she tried to hide you away."

"Are you saying you want to go back to Russia? But people all over the world already know who you are. They'll recognize you there just as they do here."

"They know the me who is dressed up and made up, and posed for the photos. They know the first lady. They don't know the Metka me. I was an ordinary person for seventeen years before I met you. I know how to be ordinary, even if you do not."

That hurt, but he could never be angry with her. She could tell him he'd failed her and that she hated him and that she could never trust him again—she could break his heart in two, in other words—and he'd still love her and understand her and forgive her whatever pain she caused him.

"You're saying your life can't work if I'm with you," he said.

Her eyes filled and she looked away. "I wish it could, believe me."

In that moment, her sorrow overflowed with the suffering she'd withstood, and Evander's throat tightened without his consent. He sought out the floor. "So you mean to go without me."

She placed her hand on his arm. "I don't want to. If there is a way we can stay together, I want that. But, I can't—"

"You would leave me." The realization left him dazed, off balance.

"For our children, Evander. You have to admit after what's happened to Natasha that it's for the best. Your family, the Jovians," she said with disdain, "they do what they have to do to get their way. They always have. Our children don't mean much to them. They do not have a 'role' to play in Caroline's grand scheme for the universe. She hardly notices them," she said with an exasperated breath. "And I want to get them out of here before she does."

Their kids were so obviously human, so imperfect, but

Nadia was right: when it came to Caroline, no one knew what she had planned, not even Evander.

He sat back in surrender, like a lump sunk into couch pillows. "I'm so sorry. I've always trusted my family and their intentions. I've never doubted them." He'd never felt more human, never felt more like his mother must have, surrounded by mysterious Jovians.

"But you doubt them now," Nadia said. "I'm sorry this is happening to you."

"Something in the grand scheme of things has changed," he said. "It's more than just what's happening to me. I can't put my finger on it. It's the first time in my life that I can't see what's ahead." His body flamed with the honesty and embarrassment of that admittance.

She shrugged and said, "Your human side seems to be rising to the forefront." The she smiled and her eyes became sad. "Welcome to my world."

He'd always sympathized with humans and their indecisiveness and insecurity, their general not-knowing. And now that he'd experienced what that felt like in its fullest form, he wanted to get away from it. He wanted the oneness back.

"I've loved you since I first met you," Nadia said, reaching up and brushing her fingers across his cheek, "but I never imagined I was stepping into this life. I've never felt I had much of a say. You needed a wife, and I was there. The Jovians welcomed me because I fulfilled a role that needed playing."

"But you know that's not all it was for me," he said. "You don't think I—"

"Of course not." She placed her fingers on his lips. "I know that you love me."

"I do, Nadia. I'm sorry for the sacrifices you've made."

"I don't regret my decisions. I've loved being your wife. But I've been unhappy for some time now. The more famous you've become, the smaller our lives have become. If I go with the children, if we can make a new home, our lives will expand, and I'll finally be making choices, for better or worse. The kids and I can be normal people who take walks and drive to the ice cream shop on a whim. I would love that. Wouldn't you?"

Their children would never be normal people, and not only because of their ailments. They were Jovian. Nadia seemed to have forgotten. She assumed because they were different from other members of the family that they merely occupied a branch on the family tree. She didn't know what it was like to be part of the oneness, but the children did, or at least they were starting to.

"Do you want a life without me in it?" he asked.

"No," she said, her face softening with apology, "but I know what I don't want, and I don't want the life I have anymore. You have important work to do, I understand that." Her hands shook as she rubbed tears from her cheeks. "If you bring Natasha home—"

"I'll bring her home," he said doing his best to sound more confident than he was. "Wherever she is, I'll find her."

She studied his face, as if reading something unsure in his expression. "You think she's far away, don't you? You think they've taken her out there, someplace in the cosmos. You know how much I never wanted that to happen. And I won't go there. If that's what the Jovians want for us, I don't care. Do not ask us to leave this planet."

"I don't know where they've taken her," he said, asserting the calm. "But it doesn't matter. Wherever she is, I'll find her and then we can talk about living somewhere else, *doing* something else."

Nadia said nothing, and he knew why. "And if you want to live apart from me, I'll understand."

"What if you don't find her?" she said.

"I will."

Nadia appeared saturated in misery, the agony of a mother's love drenching her like a woman facing a storm without so much as a raincoat. He leaned in and took her in a hug, his love for her blanketing their bodies in warmth. When they eased apart, her eyelids fluttered closed and she said, "I can't stand to be awake anymore. I'm going to bed. I don't mean to hurt you, Evander. You do know that I love you as much as I ever have?"

"Yes," he said.

"Can you bring Dmitri up in a little bit?"

"Of course I will," he said. "Sleep well. We'll talk more tomorrow."

It was agony to let her go—for her to *want* to be away from him. The pain and rejection spread from limb to limb like a living organism with writhing tentacles radiating shame and self-loathing.

As Nadia walked away, Evander beat back the urge to follow her up the stairs and promise her things would be different when Natasha came home, that he would be different and their life would change in whatever ways she wanted it to.

He couldn't make that promise because he didn't know whether something like that was even possible.

Evander sat in the near dark with Dmitri and his keys, wondering how he had arrived in this place of complete futility. He'd never failed at anything before, yet he'd failed to protect those he loved most. Was this how humans felt most of the time, and if so, how did they find the strength to carry on?

He went to the kitchen and made a cup of tea, a very

human thing to do, he realized. He returned to the garden room, sat on the couch, on the section closest to where Dmitri's upper body sprawled across the coffee table. He thought of Natasha's attempt to reach him, the strange way her words had broken into his internal space, the desperation in her voice.

He placed the tea on the coffee table, and when he sat back, he noticed Dmitri watched him and might have been watching him for some time.

"Hey, kiddo, I miss you, you know that?"

With his usual jerking movements, Dmitri pushed himself from the tabletop to the floor beside it, resuming his common position, on his back staring upward. He lifted the keys in his right hand, his arm straight, and allowed them to jingle to the beat of his infirm muscles.

"I wish we could talk the way we used to, when I could speak to you internally," Evander said, reaching out to muss Dmitri's hair. The child froze in place, eyes beaming at Evander.

Just then a sound like wind through a cracked window sped through Evander's mind and he braced himself for the possibility of forthcoming pain. He expected the speeding train with Natasha's voice trailing after, but it did not arrive. Instead, Dmitri's voice did. "But," he said and then stopped there as if struggling to form the next word the same way he would if he were speaking aloud. "We" appeared next and then there was another pause before the word "can" followed.

But we can, Evander thought.

Dmitri then spoke out loud: "Daaa-da-dy," he said, his neck retracting with the effort, his head tilting first upward and then to the side.

"Dmitri!" Evander whispered in awe. "How are you able to do this?"

His son's giggles cascaded like a rush of hopefulness inside Evander's mind.

"I . . . just . . . can." Dmitri went back to staring up at his keys.

"Can you talk to your sister this way as well?"

"No." Pause. "But I saw her go. I know who she left with."

An image barged into Evander's mind. The garden room from the perspective of the ground—Dmitri's point of view when he lay on his blanket on the floor. The back door opened, and Uncle Jimmy walked in. "There you are, my boy," he said in his jolly way. Then he crossed the room and knelt beside Natasha, who was busy with her doctor equipment, examining her favorite doll. Uncle Jimmy spoke to her in hushed words that Dmitri didn't hear. Then he placed his hand on Natasha's arm. Her face lit with excitement, and she said, "Yes!" The two of them stood and walked hand-in-hand toward Dmitri. Natasha raised her pointer finger to her lips and said, "Shhhh." Uncle Jimmy winked. "Don't you worry, my boy, we'll be back soon."

They left out the back door.

No one was there to stop them.

Dmitri's keys dropped onto the coffee table beside him, and the image faded. A stream of relief washed over Evander, but it was only a moment before a deluge of fury took its place. How dare Jimmy do this? What could he need Natasha for? She was a child. A kindergartener! *She has a heart problem.* Was there a chance Jimmy took her in order to heal her heart? With that, Evander could breathe. But if that was the reason for taking her, why steal her? Why not be up-front about it?

Dmitri was staring at him again. "Goo-ood?" he stammered.

"Yes, very good, Dmitri. Very helpful. Thank you."

"I can remember things," Dmitri said, speaking internally again.

"I know you can. You're very smart. I've missed you. Thank you for talking to me tonight. I needed to hear your voice."

"Can Great-grandmother hear us now?"

Evander thought about that. If what Caroline told him was true, the lack of communications affected her and David, though she definitely received some thoughts and messages. And what did that mean? Once again Evander wondered who or what was causing the trouble with the oneness. Who had the power to do such a thing? And how was Dmitri telepathically communicating without it?

"Do you want to talk to her?"

"I can't find her," Dmitri said. "When I try, a wall gets in the way. It's a castle wall made of stone."

"Well, you've reached me. Why don't you try her again?"

Dmitri's skinny legs jerked, and he threw an arm out and stretched his hand to his keys on the floor beside him. He released a sigh filled with strenuousness as he grasped and lifted them once more over his head. He stared at the silver metal cluster, jingling with the sway of unintended movement. After a moment, he settled and eventually became still. Silence descended upon the garden room. Time seemed to have stopped. Dmitri rolled onto his side and dropped the keys on the floor.

"I can't do it," he said, still speaking internally. "Has she gone away like Great-grandfather did?"

"No, she's still here. It's just a glitch in the system."

Dmitri's body trembled. "Gli-itch!" he said out loud, hiccupping with laughter.

"I know, it's a funny word," Evander said. "What I mean is our system of communications isn't working."

Dmitri continued to laugh, as if he couldn't stop, the way eight-year-olds often do.

"Do you talk to Great-grandmother often, Dmitri?"

His giggles segued into a humming sound, and he answered internally once again: "I'm her favorite."

"Her favorite? I thought *I* was her favorite," Evander feigned jealousy.

"Not anymore. Because I am!" The boy's face scrunched, and his crooked mouth shined with saliva as his body jerked side to side.

Evander experienced a momentary flare of pride. So Caroline did take an interest in his children—or, at least, one of them. But if that were so, why hide it? Why forge a secret relationship? Unless she was laying the groundwork for the future. Perhaps she already knew what role Dmitri would play in his lifetime.

That was it. She knew Dmitri's role the same way she'd known what she needed Evander for.

"I have no doubt you're her favorite," Evander told him. "What about your sister, does Great-grandmother talk to Natasha the way she talks to you?"

The boy moved his head side to side in jagged measures, indicating the negative. "Please put me in my bed?" he said.

"Of course," Evander spoke out loud.

He scooped his son from the floor, lifting him without trouble. Dmitri weighed about thirty-five pounds, the equivalent of a medium-size dog, one with spindly limbs that twisted around as if not solidly connected to his core. Evander still hoped that one day Dmitri would grow strong, that Jovian scientists might discover a way to treat his damaged muscles, and he would move like other people, speak with ease, and handle all of life's challenges. Or maybe he would remain the same, and that would be all right, as long as he found his way to happiness.

They passed through the kitchen and into the foyer, then up the staircase. Dmitri occupied a room on the second floor because Nadia wanted him nearby. When Evander placed him on his bed, they once again spoke telepathically: "You know how much I love you and Mommy and Natasha, don't you?" Evander asked. "You know you're the most important part of my life?"

"Mommy wants to go to Russia, but Natasha isn't home."

"I'll bring Natasha home."

"She's far away, isn't she?"

Evander gazed out the window. The stars and the moon shined overhead as if nothing at all were amiss.

"Yes, Dmitri, I'm afraid she is."

25

Fran couldn't sleep. He spent a couple of hours tossing and turning before getting out of bed and giving in to the lure of the living room screen. He swiped the remote from the coffee table and dropped onto the couch. "Turn on USN," he said.

A newscaster he'd never seen before with an even deeper voice than his own materialized, saying something about a fire on the West Coast. The fires out West had diminished to a manageable flareup every year or so, thanks to the stance Evander took on global warming. The Jovian family had done their share of good, Fran gave them that much, but the amount of power they possessed never failed to disturb him. He didn't doubt they could control all the networks and public broadcasting whenever they felt it was necessary, and this time it was imperative that they did.

Or was it? The fact that this was Fran and Max's problem a lot more than it was the Jovians' hit him like Leonard's strike to the face. If they wanted to throw him under the bus, they easily could. They could blame the whole fiasco occurring at Independence Lawn on humans. Specifically the young human named Max Vasquez.

That decided it: he, Lisa, and Max would pack up the SUV and head to the mountains. They'd find a cheap, rundown campsite without much by way of amenities, a place most campers would avoid, and stay there until further notice. Should be safe enough. Then no matter what happened, whether the Jovians stood by them or not, they would be hidden.

He'd decided to wake Lisa and Max when footage of the fire gave way to the next story in line. The news station's audio-logo crashed like cymbals, startling Fran the same way someone banging on the front door would have. BREAKING NEWS in bold black letters appeared across the bottom of a clip: the protest at Independence Lawn. Angry humans shouting and waving their fists. A shaky amateurish videographer's point of view deep in the crowd. The sea of people moved like a mosh pit, the cell phone recording jostling this way and that as the scene unfolded. A voice-over said, "What you are about to see is disturbing and unsuitable for young viewers."

"No," Fran whispered, leaning toward the television.

"Tell him to put his gun away," a deep, angry voice demanded. With sudden blurred motion, whoever held the cell whipped around 180 degrees. The camera's POV surged forward and then back until it found Fran, the arms of the chanting crowd getting in the way of a clear view. The camera, maybe ten yards away, focused on Fran's face.

"I saw it. He was waving it around."

The sound of Leonard's voice brought a shot of phantom pain to Fran's newly healed temple. He stared at the screen with glassy disbelief, vaguely aware that his mouth hung open.

"He wouldn't do that," Fran said on camera, puffing his

chest, preparing for a fight. "Do your damn job and leave us alone."

The person holding the cell phone nosedived then, the audio thumping against the ground before the video blacked out. Fran remembered Leonard pushing his way through the protesters, knocking people over as he went. He hoped that would be the end of the footage, but then the camera revived, catching some light. It trembled as it rose, glimpsing the body parts of those closest, then bumped around for a few seconds before it found Max standing on the large metal container beside an Andrew clone—with his gun drawn. The camera zoomed to Max's face—his wide, frightened eyes— and rested there. The kid perfectly identifiable.

Fran in the video shouted, "Max, run."

The cell phone recorded the release of the bullet and the subsequent way Leonard's body spewed blood. It captured those around him screaming and the crowd becoming an organism that pulled away and then snapped back, too thick and lumbering for the space that contained it. In the distance, Max jumped into the fray as if leaping from the deck of a boat into a sea of sharks.

It all happened so fast. The cell phone jumbled and shook, struggling to remain steady. The sounds of chaos overwhelmed the audio, becoming distorted and indecipherable. Finally the view jolted at a severe angle and froze on the image of a sweaty, greasy-haired woman in the midst of open-mouthed panic.

The news station returned to the anchor man in his gray suit and unemotional air. "Authorities have set up roadblocks and are conducting a search for the man who discharged the bullet that started what people are now calling the Battle of Philadelphia. He has not yet been identified but is described as a young man in his twenties, dressed in a security uniform. If you have any information, call the hotline found at the bottom of the screen. You can expect more on this story as it unfolds."

They don't have our names.

That had to be due to some Jovian magic. Both of them appeared in the film. Both of their faces, clearly pronounced. Why hadn't the Jovians stopped the footage from getting out? He couldn't dwell on that. He needed to make a new plan. There would be no way to safely drive out of Kirksberg. No way to head to the mountains and hide at a campsite, no matter how desolate.

His phone rang. A number he didn't recognize. He couldn't pick up. He wouldn't. But then something happened that had not occurred in years: Andrew's voice appeared in his mind. Andrew, his best friend. "Answer it," he said.

Was it for real?

"You can trust him," the voice said.

Fran nearly knocked the phone out of his own hand pressing the Accept button.

"Fran? Are you there? It's Evander."

Fran's chest trembled as he sucked in a breath. "Yeah, I'm here."

"You need to come to Starbright. Footage of the gunshot just aired."

"I saw it. How did that happen?"

"We think one of the security squad leaked it."

"Did Leonard survive?"

"He'll make it. With some upgrades. Andy's still working on him."

Upgrades meant robotic enhancements, which weren't a bad thing, though Leonard would end up even less person-able than he already was. Fran wondered what the other clones on the squad would think of that. Would they shrug their shoulders like it wasn't a big deal, or would they decide it was something that deserved payback? How the hell was he going to do his job?

Who was he kidding? Caroline would fire him—probably already had. He just didn't get the memo yet.

"Uh, listen," Fran said, "I don't know if coming to Starbright is the best thing."

"You'll be safe here. I'll make sure of it."

They had to go somewhere. They couldn't stay home. And Andrew just told him he could trust Evander. Either that or Fran had come down with a sudden case of schizophrenia.

"You can't drive your way out of this," Evander said, talking faster now, his usual calm clipped with urgency. "The police are searching for Max. Federal officials too. He'll be blamed for what's happening in Philadelphia."

"I know, I know, you're right. You're sure it's safe?"

"Martin's on his way in the van. The police will be there soon. You need to get out of the house. Right now, Fran."

"Okay, okay," he said.

"Just until the roadblocks disappear," Evander said. "Then you can decide what to do. I'll see you in a few minutes."

"Thanks, man." Fran was halfway to Max's bedroom. When he got there, he thumped on the door, heard Max's "I'm up" and shouted, "We have to move." Then he jogged up the stairs to the master. He found Lisa already dressed. "I just heard from Evander," he said. "We have to go now."

"Is Max up?" Lisa said.

Fran grabbed pants and pulled them on. "Help him get his stuff together. Martin will be here any second."

"Secret service Martin? Where are we going?"

"Starbright."

Lisa's brows thrust together the way they did when she was ready to argue. "Is that a good idea right now?"

"It's the *only* idea. And Evander promised we'll be safe."

Lisa still wasn't moving.

"I know it's a risk, but we have to trust him," Fran said. "We have to go. We'll make a better plan later."

She blinked with confusion. "This makes sense to me *only* because he's Svetlana's son."

"And, you know what else?" Fran said, because he couldn't wait to tell her what had just happened.

Her expression said, "tell me already."

"Andrew reached out to me just now. He flat out said, 'You can trust him.'"

"You mean, Andrew Andrew? The same way he contacted you years ago, when Svetlana needed help?"

"Yeah," Fran said, allowing himself a moment of happiness in the midst of potential catastrophe. "Son of a gun, he did."

26

The van with Martin and the Vasquez family arrived at the rear of Starbright International just as Evander's ride pulled in. He and Elsa led them through the back door, into the red room, where Evander asked them to wait while he walked to the far-left wall and located the panel near the floor. Elsa hovered over him, her white hair and pantsuit glowing red.

Fran, Lisa, and Max whispered amongst themselves while Evander pressed his thumb to the panel's middle. It then popped open, revealing a console of smooth buttons. He lay his hands on it as the code raced through his mind. With a hydraulic whine, the circular entrance to a fluorescently lit tube emerged from behind the wall.

The red lighting had shut down, and the glowing buzz of emergency lights appeared at the ceiling level.

"It's red until someone opens the tube," Fran said as if he'd just discovered one of the seven wonders of the world. "It's so you can tell if someone has breached the tube."

"Just a precaution," Evander said. "Come on, this way."

"This is so friggin' cool," Max said. "We *will* be safe here."

"You think we'd take you someplace unsafe?" Fran said.

With her perfect posture, Elsa stepped in and strode ahead, two steps in front of Evander. The tube progressed at a modest ascending angle. Sealed storage doors lined its curved sides. In an emergency situation, the Jovian family took refuge here—they had retreated to the passage several times in the past, when the media or government (the FBI, for example) took too much interest in them for whatever reason. The tubes allowed time to pass and interest to gloss over, as needed.

Evander remembered when a newspaper reporter, who also happened to be a military veteran, clearly observed and also clicked a photograph of a spacecraft with a malfunctioning camouflage system as it left Starbright headquarters. That incident required a six-month stay in captivity for the entire Jovian elite and many of the employed clones as well.

The Jovian promise, to each other and the planet, had always been to remain in the background. To guide humanity but not to demand, never to overpower. And Evander had great respect for that.

The tube's storage units housed all the family may need by way of nutrition and health, as well as pods to retreat to for comfort, leisure, and relaxation. After David appeared in his true form in the Kirksberg Park, the family spent an entire year in the tubes before Caroline and Edmund deemed it safe to so much as visit the family wing in the same building. In the meantime, business continued as usual, just not with any of the Jovian royalty present or accessible.

One of the doors opened to a second corridor, which would take them to the spaceship, in case a quick getaway became necessary.

"Does it lead to every part of the building?" Fran asked Evander.

"Most parts, if you know your way. For instance, we're

heading to the astronomical observatory. Beyond that, if we continued straight through, we would reach the greenhouse."

Max made a strange, excited sound, his lips smacking together as if he'd meant to say something but had been too flabbergasted to form words. "Oh, man, I *have got* to get up there. Do you have anything from Mars?"

"Max, please, not now," Lisa said, sharing a worried glance with Fran.

"Of course we do," Evander said, amused. "You'll have to ask Dayana for a tour sometime. She's the ruler of all things kingdom *plantae*."

"Best not to encourage him," Fran said at a low level so only Evander could hear.

Evander laughed. In many ways Max remained childlike, and that was a good quality to have. The best inventors and explorers retained their sense of playfulness and wonder, and those attributes inspired them to continue when others gave up. Max yearned to explore, that was clear.

Soon they arrived at the circular door with the carved piece of redwood that read, *"in via lactea."* Latin for "into the galaxy." Elsa stepped aside, and Evander swiped his hand over the letters, feeling its smooth, ancient grooves connect with the pads of his fingers. The door eased opened, and the white-blue light of the tube gave way to the natural light of the astronomical observatory. The early-morning sky cast a nightlight-like glow through the room's open ceiling as if entering through the pupil of a giant's eye.

Elsa stepped in first, making a quick round before Evander followed. He stood at the room's center, beside the wide, squat telescope, and watched as the Vasquez family entered the room. He felt good for a moment, as good as a parent whose child is missing can. Being with Fran's family, seeing their dedication to each other, their awe and wonder at all they were experiencing, made him hopeful. He knew Svetlana would applaud his helping them in this way.

But that's not the only reason he wanted to help. He admired Fran for the way he tried so hard to be a good father, to protect and guide his son. The man wasn't perfect, far from it, but he was honorable and respectable, and those weren't easy qualities for a human being to aspire to. Evander had been the president of a great nation, and yet he knew firsthand that being a parent was the most challenging, most important role on Earth.

Martin, the last one through, closed the door. A round table with chairs to seat five or six gathered beside the wall to the left. Evander gestured to it: "Have a seat. We'll put the news on and see what's happening."

Once the Vasquezes settled in, Evander would visit the basement. He'd already made the order to ready his transportation and needed to map out a course. Uncle Jimmy told him not to go to Io, though he didn't know why. If only they could have spoken to each other with transparency. Instinct told Evander that perhaps Jimmy wanted him to go to Mintaka. He could always start there and head to Io and Europa later. Either way, he needed to determine what Edmund had been doing all this time, and inform him of the happenings on Earth. Edmund likely knew a lot more about Caroline and the plan she was carrying out as well.

Evander glanced at the gray wash of morning sky, wishing it were midnight so he could see the stars. At least they would lend him some semblance of normalcy, some connection to the beyond.

Elsa pressed a button on the left-side wall and a curved screen unrolled from a recess there, then flickered to life. An anchorwoman dispensed the usual financial blather. "Is this okay, sir," Elsa asked. Then she became utterly still and stared blindly into space. With her ivory complexion and head cocked like a bird's, she looked a lot like something found at a department store.

"Elsa, what is it?" Evander asked.

"Yes, sir. It's—" she blinked and tilted her head at a more severe angle in the opposite direction. "We need . . ." Her lashes fluttered. "I'm getting a strong—" She stepped up to the digital screen. "Something important. I can't quite . . ."

By this time, she held everyone's rapt attention. The light-heartedness the group shared when they'd reached the safety of the tubes dropped to the floor and scattered like dried leaves.

Elsa put her hands on her temples. "It's . . . " She stopped short again.

The wall screen turned black. A soundless, empty pause followed.

Fran looked to Evander. "There's nothing there."

The screen flashed white-gray. And then again. An image appeared, the word *LIVE* in the upper right-hand corner. Independence Lawn. A dark, dismal place under charcoal clouds and imminent storm. The lampposts encircling the area twinkled dimly. Human fighters gripped wooden fence posts, the occasional stone or brick, and other weapons they'd jury-rigged from whatever materials they could get their hands on. They were mud splattered and wild, knotty haired, some of them bleeding from the mouth or nose, arm or leg.

The clones held the perimeter, looking a lot less haggard than the humans who came at them. Clean, composed, prac-tically *fresh* in their black uniforms. And plentiful. Far more plentiful than they'd been during Evander's failed speech the prior day.

Human by human, the clones chipped away at the crowd, relieved them of their stones and posts, and if necessary, took them to the ground. Once subdued, they were escorted out of the venue. It was a methodical system, simple and effective, and carried out with patience and unemotional astuteness. It was, Evander knew, the security squad's way.

The clones did their job well.

"As you can see," the anchorwoman said, "the battle between human and clone rages on. I have to point out that for the number of people involved there have been only a handful of fatalities which occurred early in the day after a gun was fired during the former president's speech. In addition, very few injuries have been reported. Do you have the specifics from the med tent, Mike?"

The camera cut to a man wearing a helmet and goggles, and a vest that resembled a shield. The battlefield spread out behind him. "Yes, Anna, I do. A total of three have suffered sprains of various sorts, and there was one head injury when a man of fifty years swung a fence post intended to hit clone. The post collided with a wall and bounced back, causing a head wound."

"Oh, wow, that was bad luck."

"Yes. He was treated for bruises and has since left the area, as so many humans have."

"Many seem to be leaving on their own accord," the anchor continued, "considering the impending bad weather."

"That's right. It's starting to rain here, and the sky has become almost as dark as night. Forecasters predict a substantial storm. More important, people are claiming exhaustion. At this point, we estimate only a quarter of the attendees remain from yesterday's peak. With temperatures dropping, we're expecting hypothermia to become an issue."

"Okay, Mike, thank you. Stay dry—"

A flash lit the screen to the point of bright white opacity, holding on like a bolt of lightning that takes its time to flame out. For a moment, nothing could be seen through the white-out. And then the screen flickered and went black, as if it had fainted.

A woman's overly loud voice crackled with distortion through the speakers. "Good morning to you all."

Whoever manned the news camera woke from unconsciousness, and the lens whipped around to face the stage. On the field, the humans put their hands over their ears. "Please turn your attention to me," the woman demanded.

The camera panned this way and that, then did a deep backbend, providing a clear view of the sky before coming back down to Earth and directing its attention to the stage. What it settled upon made Evander wither: a blonde woman in a black skirt suit. Long legs, high heels. Strict posture. The bobbed hair he knew so well.

"I am Caroline Jovian, perhaps some of you know my grandson, Evander Peterman, the former President of the United States."

A few slow claps rose from the weary crowd in an exhausted manner, and then more joined in with whatever zeal it could muster. "Bring back Evander! Bring back Evander!" wafted upward in wisps here and there.

"That's very kind of you, but as you know he has retired from the presidency," she said. "I am here to tell you that what has been happening here this week will never be allowed to happen again. I am ordering both humans and clones to stop fighting at once. Put down your weapons, and clear the lawn."

People in the crowd looked at each other with baffled shrugs and downward-turned mouths. The rain, much heavier now, continued to fall, the trampled field starting to puddle.

"Who the hell do you think you are?" one woman shouted.

"Get off the stage," said another.

That's when Miranda and Leo appeared from opposite sides of the amphitheater. They joined Caroline at the center, remaining just a step or two behind.

Caroline leaned forward, toward the mic. "Humans must leave the area immediately," she said. "Go home. Be safe."

Laughter rose from the crowd. A man with a fence post in his hand found a barrel to climb upon and shouted, "Hell no, we won't go!" Others joined in. The clones, taking advantage of the distraction, continued to disarm, apprehend, and remove those who ventured closest to the perimeter.

Caroline stared straight ahead, her demeanor as sharp and piercing as the determination in her stance. "I have asked you all to leave, and that is exactly what you will do," she said. Then she stood absolutely still . . . and waited.

Meanwhile, the clones carried the humans away, one by one by one.

Finally, with maybe one hundred stubborn protesters left on the field, Caroline said, "Well done. You are to be commended."

Who she was commending, Evander wasn't sure.

The news camera captured the wind blowing back her hair and the rain pelting the stage.

"Clones," said Caroline as if the word were a command, "my friends and protectors. I've been told that you want a promise from me. Your leader, Drew, has informed me that you are demanding your freedom. Freedom to choose the kind of life you will lead."

The camera turned away from the stage and spanned the field. It arrived at Drew, who stood on a particularly tall cargo container, his hair soaked and clinging to the sides of his face. He raised a fist and shouted through a bullhorn, "Make the promise!"

Caroline continued to gaze upon the crowd. She stared so long and hard that a taut silence spread across the field. The remaining humans stopped moving and provided their full attention.

"I don't have to promise anything," she said. "And you will soon see that for yourself."

Drew stood as tall and bold as ever, unwilling to back down. Once again he raised the bullhorn to his mouth. "Then we will no longer fight for you," he replied, his face distorted with anger, an expression like none Evander had ever seen on the face of a clone.

Caroline stepped back from the microphone. She, Miranda, and Leo formed a straight line. They grasped hands before coming together in a circle.

What in the world . . .

The spotlight that lit the trio flicked off, leaving the stage dark and shining dully with wet, dim reflections. The camera repositioned its focus upon the lawn. The human stragglers remained eerily still, and the ceaseless thrum of the downpour replaced their angry cries.

The camera fainted backward and scanned the sky above, as if it had been knocked over.

Fran said, "What's going on? Why's the cameraman doing that?"

The anchorwoman's voice appeared for the first time in a long while: "Mike, can you tell us what's happening? It's hard to grasp what we're looking at."

"Uh, sure, let me just . . . " Mike said, his voice laced with static that sounded screechy and awful. "There's some kind of movement onstage. A dim glow that's, uh, hard to describe, and a strange electricity in the air. I can't tell what . . ." His voice was barely decipherable, a mere zap of words, like a person speaking through a kazoo. "The cloud coverage has thickened to a severe degree and—"

Thunder steamrolled overhead.

Suddenly the camera's view blurred. It gradually recovered, homing in on something not on the stage but in front of it, on the lawn. Something very black, smooth . . . *enormous*. The camera lens rediscovered focus, and Evander held his breath.

What he saw was Jovian.

In Jovian form.

Streamlined and featureless.

An alien on Earth.

On a field in Philadelphia.

Caroline?

The transition had taken her to her knees, and she appeared on all fours, her body the equivalent of two or three of the historic homes that made up Liberty Square.

The hundred or so humans remaining on the field scattered, pushing clones aside as they rushed for the exits. But the clones maintained their posts, standing guard as they had for days.

"What the hell?" Fran said.

This is not happening, Evander thought.

Lisa grabbed Max and pulled him close as if needing to protect him from the thing on the screen.

"Is that . . . Caroline?" Fran said. "Evander? Is that your grandmother?"

Evander couldn't respond.

The alien rose upon her massive legs, a gigantic queen with a huge, smooth oval head. Her limbs, elongated and black, shined sleek and smooth as the paint on a brand-new car. The TV image of her proved not quite solid from one second to the next; the camera failed to capture her likeness in a normal way. The image of her blurred and shimmered around its edges, and gave her an overall unreal appearance as if her overwhelming energy foiled human technology.

Evander drew in a shaky breath. *Grandmother, what have you done?*

The others in the room gasped and murmured. Fran grumbled, "That has to be Caroline."

Evander remained in his own head.

The camera surveyed the field and found Drew wearing a blank, robotic countenance. His body stood stiff and unmoving, bent at the waist as if seized in the midst of motion. The camera panned along the line of clones, all of them in the same physical state: paralyzed like mannequins.

Evander heard Caroline in his mind, just as, no doubt, the clones did. "You will defend this planet," she said. "It is your duty to do so. There is no choice. This is the role you were meant to play. This is what you were born to do. And you will do it."

The only way she could voice these commands internally was through the oneness.

Which was why Evander heard her loud and clear while the television—and the venue in Philadelphia—remained silent.

The giant alien towered above the lawn, and the camera tipped back to capture as complete a view as possible. Caroline's legs extended like the trunks of trees, the whole of her shimmering black. She brought her hands in front of her and pressed them together. Her large head tipped back slightly, then forward. She pulled her hands apart and then struck them together. The resulting clap shook the camera and vibrated for seconds afterward like a tremor of aftershock.

The clones snapped to: feet together, shoulders back, arms and legs straight.

Caroline dropped her chin, and they fell into perfect lines.

"You are my army," she told them. "I have brought you into this world for this reason. This is my supremacy. My power. I control you with the oneness of my family. And I always will." Her voice charged through Evander's head, and he knew the clones were hearing the same thing. "When we're finished here, you'll go back to your lives. From this day forward you will be dedicated to your duty. Dedicated to *me*. There will be no more protests. You have a role to play, and you will play it."

The alien stepped forward, her immense weight shaking the ground the camera stood upon. She bent to one knee, reached into the line of clones standing before her, and took one of them into her hand. The camera zoomed in, and Evander saw that it was Drew. Caroline lifted him like a doll from the ground before rising once again upon her broad legs. She plucked the tiny bullhorn from his hand and tossed it away, then walked back to the amphitheater and placed Drew on the stage. He stood and stared at her without expression.

The rain came down, and thunder growled in the distance. Caroline remained present for a moment longer, a shiny black, not-quite-decipherable image framed at the center of the digital screen while lightning flashed around her.

Very slowly, very gradually she became one with her surroundings. No human on Earth, except maybe Evander or his father, Andrew, would have been able to see her retreat in this way.

To everyone else, she simply disappeared.

Evander grabbed his head and doubled over, his mind awash with a ferocious wave of voices as the full power of the oneness reentered his consciousness. A chaotic mix of thoughts reared up with such strength and volume, he feared his head would explode. Like a wave, however, the deluge broke upon the shores of his mind, crashed over the landscape, and gradually receded. As it pulled back, he became aware that he lay on the ground, and Elsa stood over him. The Vasquezes hovered in frightened silence a few feet away.

"He's still with us," Elsa said. "Blood pressure normal. Oxygen low. Martin, where's that tank?"

Martin handed her an oxygen tank and a clear face mask to go with it. Elsa pressed the mask to Evander's face, and he breathed in and tried to relax. He startled when Uncle Jimmy's voice broke through the oneness. "I have her," he said. "I have Natasha. She's safe. We can help her, Evander. I'm sure of that now. I'm sorry. . . . What I did . . . couldn't be . . ." A lapse in connection passed and then Evander heard, *"Natasha must live."*

He shivered, and the hair on his scalp prickled. Uncle Jimmy's words overwhelmed his rational mind. He squeezed his eyes closed and struggled to reply. "Where are you?" he said through the oneness.

"Mintaka. I tried to tell you. Mintaka!"

"I couldn't hear you. I could hardly hear Natasha. How did she get through?"

"She's stronger than you know, Evander."

The answer struck him as ominous—and he hoped it was true.

"Caroline disabled the oneness," Evander said. "And David is overburdened. It's possible he tried to stop her but couldn't."

"I saw what happened," Jimmy said. "When Caroline took her true form, the oneness snapped back into place. I don't know how long it will last. She doesn't want us to communicate. But you're wrong about one thing: Caroline isn't responsible for the trouble with the oneness. It was Edmund who disabled communications."

"Edmund? But why?"

"He left Earth because he and Caroline disagree on the

way forward. She wants to rule from the forefront, no longer from the shadows. That's why she wants you to leave. That's why she showed her true form today. It's no longer enough for her to rule through the presidents she has chosen. She wants all the power. She wants to be queen."

"That can't be true," Evander said. For as long as he'd known her she'd wanted the best for Earth. She loved this bright blue planet.

A zapping sensation buzzed within his skull and Evander felt the strength of their connection wane. "Uncle Jimmy, stay with me."

Strange metallic sounds stirred in Evander's mind, mixed with bits of conversation, some of it Uncle Jimmy, some unknown voices. " Edmund traveled to Io . . . organizing the Moon Children . . . Caroline . . . attack . . . imminent. . . humans and clones."

The oneness rose and dipped like a ribbon undulating in erratic wind. "Come t . . . taka . . . We . . . need . . . oo."

"Tell Natasha I love her," Evander said as forcefully as he could.

Uncle Jimmy's final words came to him in a whisper: "She must live."

The oneness ceased, and Evander lay back, exhausted, his ears ringing.

The digital screen on the wall showed the clones as they dropped to their knees in unison. Once released, they glanced about, confused, then rose to their feet and scattered, desperate to get away.

27

The news anchor shouted "What the hell is going on? Is this real? What kind of crazy sh—" The network cut to a "Technical Difficulties" screen.

Fran startled out of his shock when Lisa grabbed his hand and squeezed so tight his fingertips smarted. "I'm so sorry," she said. "I'm sorry I ever doubted you. If I hadn't seen it myself, I might never have believed—"

A few feet away, Elsa and Martin tended to Evander.

"It's okay," Fran said. He opened his arms around her and Max, and shuffled them farther away for privacy.

Lisa had never believed what he'd try to tell her about the Jovians and their natural form. But now she knew without a doubt that he had not been mistaken. Caroline had shown her true self. The entire world saw it on TV, or soon would. Eventually, mankind would figure out that aliens occupied the earth and had done so for a long, long time.

And now Fran watched the guilt weigh on his wife. Her rounded shoulders slouched as if she wore her remorse like a wet blanket across her shoulders.

"Can you ever forgive me?" she asked.

He half-smiled. "I never held it against you. It's unbeliev-able, I know that."

She hugged him, and he felt her breath in his ear. "I wanted to believe you, but I never really did, and now that I do . . . should we be here? I mean, this is *their* headquarters." She gazed in the direction of Evander and his loyal AIs. "Are we safe? He's Jovian and those other two are part human, part AI."

"They're what?" Max practically shouted. "Elsa and Martin?"

"You saw what Martin can do," Fran whispered. "And how many humans do you know have eyes like Elsa's?"

"Oh my God, what about Evander?" Max said before Fran could put a hand over his mouth. "Do you think he's like Caroline?"

Fran's fierce shake of his head stopped Max from saying more. "He's not."

The screen on the wall popped back on in the midst of a clip from the Battle of Philadelphia. Apparently it was easier to discuss news from earlier in the day than it was to describe what the world may or may not have just seen. But that wasn't good, Fran knew, especially when the station jumped to a story that broadcast Max's photo with the words "Man Hunt" in a banner below.

Young Max in the photo grinned boldly. His youthful, thick-lashed innocence, without a hint of malice, belied whatever harsh images the words underneath implied.

"Where did they get that picture?" Lisa said. "You look so young."

"Ugh. I think I'm gonna throw up," Max said.

"Is that your college ID?" she said.

His lips quivered, and he seemed to struggle to get out the word *yes* before hanging his head and making a gagging sound.

Lisa patted his back and whispered assurances in his ear. Fran scanned the room for a garbage pail Max could heave into.

The anchorwoman reported: "Authorities have connected this man to Starbright International. During the former president's speech, Max Vasquez fired a gun into the crowd and struck a fellow officer of security, thereby starting what the media is calling The Battle of Philadelphia. As you can see in the following footage, his uniform bears the Starbright Security Squad patch."

A clip from the prior day's video played in darker hues, a circle of light highlighting Max's chest and the company patch sewed into his uniform.

Max finally stood up straight, his complexion gray and sickly. "Now they're gonna come here," he said, his chin trembling. "We'll have to leave. No one is safe because of me."

"It's okay, Max," Fran said. "After what Caroline just did, I don't think they'll be here anytime soon. Besides, by law they can't enter Starbright property. And the security squad won't let them."

Max grabbed his head. "I'm such an idiot!" He turned and rushed toward the exit to the tube, tried to pull the door open, then groaned with frustration when he couldn't. "Can I get out of here, please? I need to be alone for a minute."

Evander, resting in a chair on the opposite side of the room, nodded at Elsa, who strode over and placed her hand on the knob. For a moment both her hand and the knob seemed to have become one, and then the door opened and Max, with a fearful expression, passed through.

Fran and Lisa exchanged a look before Fran said, "Leave it open just one more second," and took off after Max.

The kid could have run track had he any inclination to "do school sports" back in the day: he had already covered the distance ahead.

"Max, wait up. Where're you gonna go? No one can get into Starbright. You don't have to worry."

"I can't stand it. Why did it have to be me?" he shouted back.

I knew I never should've given him the job.

"It's not your fault!" Fran panted out the words as he struggled to keep up.

"All I do is make problems. I'm always the one who screws up!"

The tube ascended at a moderate degree, that much was clear, as Fran's shins began to burn. He'd thought he was in better shape than this. He slowed and dropped his head, needing a moment to catch his breath.

The sound of Max's footsteps dimmed, then disappeared. He must have reached the end of the tube. A door opened with a click but didn't close. When Fran reached it, he passed through, and it closed behind him. Maybe Elsa was working her magic from the other room.

The warm damp of the greenhouse made him sweat. He bent over once again and caught his breath, feeling thick and tired and out of shape. The wood floor below his feet resembled that of an old backyard shed, sprinkled with small pebbles and soil and twigs. It was quiet there. Tables lined up in rows, displaying plant specimens in tubs and pots, the leaves of trees and bushes crowded into the space so they formed a small but thick jungle. The air smelled of wet earth, and if someone had blindfolded him and told him they'd dropped him in the wilderness, he would have believed it. All kinds of unusual trees and ferns, mosses and mushrooms spread before him. Fuzzy and thick, blue and orange and . . . you name it. Every color and texture. Tall palms like fountains burst from the crowd here and there as did cacti with spike-like arms and little fingers at the ends. Bright yellow stalks, rust-colored branches, and black flower blossoms mixed in with leaves of silver and maroon.

"Max?" he called as he started down the center aisle. "Where'd you go?"

"Over here, Dad. You won't believe what I found. This place is so cool."

He followed the sound of Max's voice, rounding a right turn, where Max came into view sitting on a typical park bench, some kind of brown blob in a clay pot on his lap.

"What the heck is that? Is it *alive?*"

If Fran had to compare it to something on Earth, he'd say it was an obese seahorse the size of a human newborn that someone had pressed into a red-clay pot of weird spongy soil.

"The label says it's from Europa. You know, one of Jupiter's moons." Max poked gently at its roots, some of which peeked up from the soil. "I'm pretty sure it would live by the sea in its natural habitat. Europa has an icy surface, but scientists discovered an ocean underneath."

"I'll take your word for it." Fran shrugged.

"Of all the moons and small planets in our solar system, scientists believe Europa and Io might actually be habitable."

"Uh-huh." Jupiter and its moons was not the topic Fran wanted to discuss. "Look, Max, I know you don't believe this right now, but we're going to be okay. We'll figure this out."

Max frowned and returned his attention to the plant.

"Time will pass," Fran continued, "and people will forget what happened on Independence Lawn. All they'll remember is that a huge alien appeared and made the clones retreat."

"That's not true. I shot someone. I started a battle."

"That's what the media is calling it, but it was hardly a battle. Humans tried to fight and were rendered useless by clones. The only people who got hurt, hurt themselves. Don't worry, this will become something you can deal with. I promise."

"I don't want to have to deal with it," Max said. "Nothing changes on this planet. Humans and clones and Jovians, they're all set in their ways. We're programmed for failure and unhappiness."

"Come on, Max. That's not fair. I'm happy. At least most of the time. I love my life with you and your mother. And you're not always sad, either."

Max put the plant down on the bench in between them. He crossed his arms over his chest and looked straight ahead, probably to avoid Fran's parental concern. "It's just too hard," he said. "The things that make me happy aren't accessible to me. They're out there. I can see them, but I can't reach them. I'm too young or I didn't get the right degree, or NASA won't hire me until I beat out five thousand other avionics technicians and jump through three hundred hoops. I know exactly how those clones feel. How they're dying to do something they're not allowed to do."

Fran sighed because he wasn't sure how to respond. Max was right: the job he wanted, the life he desired, neither one of them would "just happen." He'd have to make them happen, and that would take time.

"I want to start living my life now, not twenty-five years from now. Otherwise, what's the point?"

"I get what you're saying," Fran said with a slow nod. "We all feel like that in the beginning, but you'll find your way. You don't get to call the shots straight out of the gate. That's just how it is for everybody. You need to have patience. No one likes waiting for the good stuff in life."

Fran lifted the plant, taking a closer look at its scaly fish-like skin. "Is this really the kind of thing that fascinates you?"

"Everything having to do with space fascinates me," Max

said, gazing at the glass roof above their heads. "Isn't it obvious?"

"Well, yeah, I mean, I know you always had space posters and read books about distant planets, but I thought all kids did that."

Max turned toward him and exhibited a maturity he rarely displayed. "This is more than some little-kid obsession." He paused, mired in thought. "You know, I was never an A student, never good at school. Sitting in class all day, staring at a teacher or a book, that didn't work for me. I always had too much energy, always wanted to be doing something else. I went into avionics because the universe interests me, and that was the best I could do, my foot in the door. What I really want is to rocket into space and explore the unknown, live on a space station, collect plant samples from places like Jupiter and beyond. All my life, that's been my dream."

As much as Fran wanted to pretend he didn't just hear what Max said, he couldn't. It was out there. His son had made it plain.

"I didn't know that was the plan," Fran said, reveling in a small spark of pride. "I thought you would end up working at a spacecraft manufacturing plant, or something."

The kid meant business and that was refreshing to see. Problem was, a familiar, darker feeling rushed in behind that swell of pride, a feeling that clutched Fran's back and neck muscles, and made him dread the future. How long would it be before Max learned more about Starbright's travelers? How long before he took off in a spaceship and possibly didn't come back?

"I get the feeling you don't like this career choice for me," Max said. "But why not? What's wrong with going out there and studying the universe?"

"No, that's not it—it's just, you know, it's a dangerous profession."

"But these days the rockets are so safe. And I'd only be the guy repairing and maintaining electronic systems."

"Well, yeah, but . . . just the whole going-to-outer-space thing in general . . ." Fran's words petered out.

Space travel is what concerned him, but he couldn't say it. He wanted to avoid those words specifically.

"I wasn't kidding when I told you I want to travel," Max said, once again going straight to where Fran wished he wouldn't go. "Going places far, far away. That's what I want. Especially after what happened on Independence Lawn."

"Yeah, I know," Fran said with a sigh. "Believe me, I know you better than you think."

"There's no future for me here." Max's voice, traveled through Fran's ears and pierced his soul. "I shot someone. The authorities are hunting me. I've never felt like I belonged here, anyway. I've never wanted to be here."

Fran looked away because he didn't understand why his son felt this way, but also because he couldn't deny that he did. The kid came out of the womb complaining, had never played well with others, quit every activity he'd ever excelled at, never pursued what Fran and Lisa encouraged him to pursue. And then, in young adulthood, he'd spent his days wearing an off-white robe and hiding in his room.

When Fran found the strength to face him, Max remained right there, a serious ready-for-anything steeling his face.

"Okay," Fran said. "I guess I'd just been hoping all these years that that would change."

"Well, it hasn't," Max said. "Every night I dream about getting off this planet. I *want* to travel. And I know the Jovians go to Jupiter all the time. Leonard told me the day I started working here. I didn't believe him until now. Because after seeing that giant alien, it's not so hard to believe anymore."

What else could Fran do but agree? His foot nudged something that tumbled gently across the ground. A pinecone. One of the miniature ones with light-brown scales. He lifted it, brought it up to the light and took note of its patterned spiral. "Are you sure you want to be part of that world? Doesn't it scare you to know what we know?"

"It does a little," he said with sober honesty. "But I still want to go."

Fran dropped the little pinecone into his shirt pocket. "I'm sorry I didn't take you seriously before. My intention was to protect you, to keep you from making mistakes. But now I see that you know what you want. And, I mean," he took a shaky breath that made him realize how hard he'd been fighting against this acknowledgment, how badly he'd wanted to change Max's mind, "you have to follow your dreams."

Though Fran was glad to have finally had this long-overdue conversation, something had broken inside of him in order to make it possible, something that concerned him and left him shaky and unsure. *Surrender isn't always relief,* he thought.

Max lay his hand on Fran's shoulder. "Don't look so sad. You're a great father, the best a kid could ask for. You haven't done anything wrong. This is just how I am. This is what I really want."

"What about your mother? You know she isn't going to like it."

"She knows about it. We've had a few talks."

"Oh, well, that's . . . good," Fran said stiffly, feeling left out and like maybe Max found him inflexible compared to Lisa, maybe even unapproachable like his own father had been. He'd never wanted to be that way. He'd promised himself a long time ago that when he had a kid of his own, he *wouldn't* be that way. And yet, maybe he had been. But it wasn't too late to change.

"Okay, so we'll have to talk to Evander," he said, "and see if he thinks you're a suitable candidate for the traveler program. I imagine there are a few years of training involved, and a lot of studying, too. It's all confidential, so I'm just guessing, but I'm sure you have to prepare—and qualify."

"Whatever it is, I'll just be happy to get started."

"If that's what you really want," Fran said, thinking, *Maybe when he finds out more about it, he'll change his mind.*

"It *is* what I want," Max said. "One hundred percent."

And there it was: stars in his son's eyes. Glimmering, sparkling stars, the very start of what Fran hoped would be Max's bright future. Fran reciprocated with a smile, though the sad part of him that lay at the center of his chest tugged at his heart with agonizing strength. *Kids*, he thought, *first they kill you with their neediness, and then, just when you think they're turning into OK, independent people, they kill you again by leaving you.*

"Okay," he said, "now put that seahorse back where you found it. We need to get back."

28

F ran and Max returned just as Elsa and Martin deemed Evander of sound mind and body—and not a second too soon.

"All right, everyone," Evander said, with renewed strength and determination. "I don't want to alarm you, but Caroline and the others are likely heading back as we speak. While she appeared in her true form, the Jovian oneness momentarily returned. I now know where my daughter is and what I have to do to reach her."

Fran and Max exchanged surprised glances.

Fran said, "That's great."

"Martin has gone to the basement to prepare my transportation."

"Holy crap!" Max said. "Is it a spaceship? Is there a frickin' spaceship in the basement?"

"Yes, there is. A lot more than one, actually." Evander winked at him.

"And you're leaving today?" Max seemed to have forgotten his own troubles. "You are, aren't you?"

"Yes, I am."

"What about your wife and Dmitri? Are you leaving them behind?"

Leaving them behind? Evander thought.

"Max, stop," Fran said, grabbing his son's shoulder. "It's not our business. I'm sorry, Evander, after seeing Caroline and everything else today, he's not himself right now."

"It's fine," Evander said, but Max's question had already tossed him back to the prior night. After his talk with Dmitri, he'd entered the master bedroom where Nadia slept. He changed into pajamas—something he hadn't done in some time, considering he didn't often need to sleep—and climbed into bed beside her. She faced away from him, and he wrapped his arms around her and observed the stress in her jaw. He took her in a full body hug, absorbing what he could of her worry and pain, her despair seeping into his chest before it flamed for a moment like a fire struggling against the blanket that snuffed it out.

Nadia's body relaxed into his arms, and she whispered, "Did you find her?"

"She left with Uncle Jimmy. I'll bring her back. I promise."

She turned to face him with a crumbling sadness he longed to alleviate. "Can they help her, can they fix her heart? The Jovians, I mean. Out there."

"I think so, yes," he said, though he felt as unsure as ever.

She put her arms around him and pulled him close, breathing full breaths of relief before her tears arrived. The fact that he and his family brought this trouble and sadness upon her tore at Evander from the inside. "I'm so sorry it's come to this," he said.

"I know you are," she told him. "Bring her back to me, okay?"

He took in a deep breath and said, "I will."

Soon after their conversation, he left the house, and now he'd be leaving the planet.

"My family is not coming with me," he told Max, "but I'll need a worthy technician on this trip, and if it's okay with your parents, I'd like to offer you the job."

Fran jerked back and at first laughed, thinking it a joke. A second later, however, Max jumped in celebration, and shouted, "Yes! I had a feeling. Thank you, Evander. Thank you!"

"Uh, wait a minute." Fran raised his hand and waved. "Doesn't Max need some training or preparation before he heads into the—"

Evander breathed in deeply and then out, imparting the calm Fran needed to survive this conversation. "He needs nothing but the desire to go," he said. "He's as prepared as he needs to be."

Fran's shocked expression faded, and he seemed to be able to think after that. "Okay, well, obviously he's more than willing."

"Listen," Evander turned to him and Lisa, "you still have a few minutes to talk it over. There will be other chances, if you decide now's not the time. That said, with what happened yesterday, it seems like a good opportunity for Max to disappear for a while."

"I don't know." Fran dropped his chin before looking to Lisa. Perhaps he hoped she would squash the idea.

"I hate to admit it," she said, "but I think he's ready. He's been ready for a while now. And it couldn't be better timing."

"But he'll be leaving *today*," Fran said. "Right now."

"I realize that, honey." Lisa placed her hand on Fran's back, "but he's not happy here. We know that. It would be different if the authorities weren't out there looking for him. If he stays, he could end up in jail." She opened her eyes wide. "We can't risk that. And look how happy he is," she said, gesturing in the direction of Max, who fired off question after question to Elsa, who couldn't answer fast enough. "We have to give him this opportunity to find some meaning in his life. This is what he wants. This is his chance to make a happier life."

Evander nodded. "And you're both more than welcome to come with us."

Max spun around, unable to camouflage his exhilaration. "Dad! Mom! You have to come with us."

"I can't," Fran said, a knee-jerk reaction. "I can't do it. I'm too old and—"

"Dad doesn't even like to fly in airplanes, honey," Lisa said with a sober laugh. "And I agree with him. If you're going to do this, you're doing it without us. We'll be here when you get back."

Elsa started for the tube entrance on the opposite side of the room. That was Evander's cue to get a move on. "I'm sorry to rush ahead," he said, "but we need to get to the basement."

Evander took the lead, walking like a man late for a flight at the airport. The Vasquezes followed behind: Max exclaimed how great all of this was and thanked both his parents for letting him go. Lisa imparted mom wisdom, like "Be sure to do your share of the work. Take proper care of yourself. Sleep well." Then she hesitated, and Evander heard the surge of emotion crowd out her next words: "Be a good person, okay? Just be a good person."

"And be smart," Fran said with a gruff edge. "Use common sense."

"I won't be gone for long," Max said. "And I'll be with Evander. He wants to get back as soon as possible."

That's when Lisa coughed out a cry. "I was going to say be sure to write, but is it possible to get messages home?"

"Hey, Evander, will Max be able to contact us?" Fran asked.

Evander turned partway around as he continued to walk.

"Not in the usual ways, but I'll be sure to get word to you. Elsa will be with me, of course, and Martin will stay here. There's an open line between them." *More consistent than the Jovian oneness at this point,* he thought.

"That's good." Fran sounded preoccupied like a man overwhelmed with thoughts.

As they continued through the tube, Evander placed his hand on Fran's shoulder, giving him another dose of calm. "It'll be a good learning experience for him. He'll grow up. Isn't that what you want?"

"I do," Fran said, "but not too much. I mean, I still want to be older than he is when he returns." An anxious laugh escaped his lips.

"Of course," Evander said.

They reached yet another door, the entrance to a docking station. It opened to a platform similar to those in the subway. When the time was right, they would board the ship through a pair of elevator-like doors. In the meantime, the blue overhead lights and eerie vibration worked their numbing magic, and even Max began to speak slower and use lower volume as he grilled Martin with questions about the ship. Behind them, the station unfolded like a parking garage void of vehicles.

Fran scanned the surrounding area and said, "It's so different from what I remember."

"Because we're in a different part of the basement," Evander explained. "We're not taking one of the larger ships."

Elsa stood beside Evander. "Shall we enter?" she gestured to the sliding doors. "Caroline and her party are expected any second now, and it may be best to avoid—"

The doors pulled apart, and Max and Lisa rushed through. Evander heard the sound of heels against the platform floor behind him.

"You've decided to leave after all."

He turned, knowing who he'd find there.

So, he'd have to face Caroline. And what would she do? Would she try to stop him from leaving now that she'd shown the world her true self? All along, she'd wanted him out of the way. He knew that for sure now.

And yet there she stood. Alone. In human form. A well-proportioned, attractive specimen of an older woman decked out in designer clothing and expensive jewels—rare gems from her favorite bright blue planet. She was the picture of health. The same Caroline he'd always known and trusted.

"Show them to the pods, Martin," Evander said. "I'll be there in a moment." To Fran, he said, "I'll take care of Max like he's one of my own. Go on in, say your goodbyes."

Fran hesitated as he glanced at Caroline. "Are you sure? I can stand by if you need me."

Elsa appeared behind them. "That's my job."

"Thank you, Fran," Evander said. "Oh, and Fran, I'm glad I got to know you as well as I have. My mother was right about you."

"Back at ya," he said, and he strode away, hurrying to catch the others.

Evander turned to face Caroline. "Grandmother."

"You've decided to join Edmund, I assume."

"What do you mean by *join*?"

She stared blank-faced as usual. Confusion and interest and praise all looked the same on her.

"You had the oneness working for a short time," he said, "so I assume you know where I'm going and why. On the other hand, I don't know why you've made the choices you've made. I wish you had let me in on your plan. I could have helped you come to a peaceful resolution without turning to drastic measures. I can still help smooth things over, if you like."

Her clipped words arrived like a reprimand: "I have no need for your help. The plan has never changed."

"Then why did you show yourself?"

Self-assurance oozed from her pores. "I saw no other way."

That was bullshit.

"Revealing the Jovian presence has never been part of the plan," Evander said boldly. "The family was to stay in the background. Our duty is to help, not to interfere, not to demand. Certainly not to frighten and dominate. The goal is to grow a strong planet populated by a strong race." He stopped there, taking a moment to tame the emotion writhing inside of him. "So, why did you do it?"

Everything about her face gave the impression of being pleased. There was no distress in the form of wrinkles around her eyes or mouth, no furrowed brow, no tension in her jaw. Just a beautiful older face, at peace with the circumstances. "You're an intelligent human," she said, "and I've always admired you for it."

"I'm also Jovian," he said, in no mood for flattery. "Let's not forget."

She reached out and touched his hand, expressing her admiration, or possibly her pride. "I never could." She'd seldom shown affection, and he'd forgotten what it was like to be in her good favor. To have her focus upon him, whether in person or via the oneness. His whole life, until five months ago, she'd made him feel special.

"Still," she said, "I'm afraid you can't see the whole picture, no fault of your own."

He'd never be good enough for her. Never Jovian enough. She no longer cared to know his opinions, his suggestions for where to go from here. Heat pooled in his cheeks, and he experienced an urge to shake her, to shout at her, *Why are you doing this? Why are you splitting the family? Who have you become?*

Instead he said, "Help me to understand. I *want* to understand. You're my family. You've always meant so much to me. Ever since I was a child, I've loved and trusted you."

"If that's true, then it should be enough for me to tell you that I did what I had to do," she said, her confidence like a brick wall in which his doubts collided headfirst. Her posture remained as self-assured as ever. She suffered no guilt, no emotions whatsoever. She was a six-story giant in the body of human female. Invincible.

And all at once, Evander knew for sure: she wasn't going to tell him any more than she already had. He'd played his part. She was as good as done with him and had already told him in no uncertain terms that she didn't need him anymore. Until that moment, it had never occurred to him that he would one day lose his seat opposite Caroline at the conference table.

For the first time in his life, he'd been fully rejected.

"You know what your problem is?" he said, his voice laced with venom. "You've never understood humans. You showed yourself today because you thought it was the only way. But there were countless actions you could have taken. You felt the situation getting out of hand, and the humans did things you didn't expect. They proved their strong will, their willingness to fight, their willingness to make peace. And you didn't know what to do about that. So you forced your way in. You showed the clones they'll never have free will, and you scared the humans to such a drastic degree that they're sure to bow to your every whim from this day forward. With one bold act, you've changed your precious bright blue planet forever.

"You realize that, don't you?" he said. "There's no going back after this. And this is *not* how it was supposed to be."

She took a step back and blinked. "The goals are the same. It matters little how we attain them."

"You don't really believe that," he said, shaking his head.

She didn't respond.

"Well, I disagree," he continued. "I believe that how we attain them matters most of all. You hold the power, you always have, and your actions have become reckless. This is *not* what we do. This is *not* how Jovians lead."

She straightened her spine so she became just a bit taller than before. "I know you disagree. I always knew you would. That's why I want you to leave."

"I assume you and Edmund couldn't find common ground," he said.

"That's right."

"About what, exactly?"

She stared. Unwilling to tell.

"And now you want me to join him? See, that's what I don't understand. I would think you'd want me to understand your point of view. I would think you'd try to convince me that whatever you're doing is the right thing."

"I know I can't do that," she said.

"You could try."

She reached out with her eyes. "You know how much I care for this planet, Evander."

"But not its inhabitants."

"The *planet* must thrive," she said, standing her ground. And then, with what Evander thought might be a gesture of empathy, she reached out with one hand and let it hover in front of him. It was as if she wanted to touch him one last time but was unable to do it. Instead she brought her arms together and folded them over her chest. "One day it will become clear to you," she said.

That wasn't good enough.

"The planet is thriving in great part due to the humans,"

he said. "I did my job. I led them through it. The humans helped make it happen."

"They're dangerous," she said. "They can't be trusted."

Now he was getting somewhere.

"Why do you feel that way? Is it because they have free will? Because you can't control their minds the way you control the clones'?"

"Yes. That's why," she said glaring at him. "They cannot be controlled. They cannot be trusted. They're no longer the dominant species on this planet, and you can't change that. The human race as you know it will die, and you must stay out of it."

"I can't do that."

"Because you made a promise to your mother?" she said.

"It's an entire species, Grandmother. A species I care deeply about. Why don't you?"

She paused, perhaps to gather her thoughts. Or maybe her courage, though she had never lacked courage before. "When your mother gave birth to you, it was both the best and the worst thing to happen to our family. You were everything I'd ever hoped for. A human child with Jovian blood, Jovian brain, Jovian gifts. A human child who would grow to have children of his own. The start of a new, *better* human being."

"I didn't ask to be the first hybrid."

"And yet that is exactly what you are. A hybrid who has chosen his human mother over the family that worked so hard to bring him into being."

He didn't know what to say to that. The ground vibrated below his feet. The transport for his trip had powered into a lower gear.

"I don't blame you for choosing Svetlana over the family," she said. "You're half human. It's only natural you should feel an attachment to her."

And you will never understand humans, he thought.

"It's true that I wanted Svetlana out of the way. But I let her stay as long as she did for your sake. I put up with her for a time, allowing her to raise you away from us, the two of you on your own. That turned out to be a mistake because during your time with your mother, you indulged your human side. And now your emotions are getting in the way. You refuse to let go, and because of that, you and I must go our separate ways."

"We don't have to," he said, hoping he may yet convince her, but then he saw something. Something that might have been there before but he'd refused to see. A streak of darkness beyond her blank stare.

"You will never see your mother again," she said. "She will never know whether you kept your promise. She won't even know if the sun rose the day after she left our universe, or if you produced offspring during your lifetime, or if the earth survived or became a dead planet the way Mars and Venus went before it. She will never know any of these things, and yet you cling to your promise to her. You are keeping a promise to a ghost. You realize that, don't you?"

"It's called loyalty," he said without hesitation. "I love my mother, no matter where she is, living or dead."

Once again, Caroline stood without speaking, without so much as blinking. "Jovians are loyal."

"I've trusted you my whole life," he said. "Is it so easy to toss me aside?"

"We no longer share common ground."

He nodded. "There's more to life than common ground."

They held a look in which he ventured deep into her eyes, beyond the pretty golden flecks, to the darker streak he sensed within her, a place where he found her shadowy animosity and black stubbornness. The ambition she once kept under lock and key.

KIM CATANZARITE

"Your time on Earth is over, I'm afraid," she said.

Every molecule of oxygen, every rushing red blood cell, every thought in a long line of endless thoughts stalled inside of him, and Evander knew, body and soul, that Caroline would never stop. She wanted it all. And worse, she feared he might prevent her from getting it. "You don't mean that," he said. "My *family* is here. I will return. I'm not leaving for long."

"Goodbye, Evander," she said.

"Are you saying you'll stop me from coming home?"

"I'm not saying anything I haven't said before."

He shook his head. He hated leaving like this, with so many unanswered questions and nothing resolved. But what else could he do? Not going wasn't an option. Nothing could stop him from finding Natasha.

"I hope that we'll speak again when I return," he said and waited for her response, unsure of what any of this meant for the future.

"I don't know if we will," she said softly, the same way a human who felt bad might say it. Most likely it was for show. Remorse was foreign to her. She wasn't sorry about any of this. Her concerns were simple. Driven. One-track.

She turned and walked in the opposite direction. So he turned too, heading for the doorway that led to the spaceship, determined not to look back, determined to keep moving forward, still puzzled as to why in the world she would rather send him away and encourage him to join her adversaries than invite him to be an ally, a bridge between two incompatible factions.

The tube flickered as the transport whirred in a familiar way. It had been twelve years since he'd traveled. He didn't want to leave Nadia and Dmitri, but he'd do anything to retrieve his daughter and reunite his family.

He entered the ship hovering in its dock, and lingered a

few feet from where Fran and Max and Lisa huddled in a tight hug, clinging to one another as if their lives depended on it. Fran took something from his pocket—a small pinecone—and handed it to Max. "Don't forget where you come from," he said, and they hugged one last time.

Caroline didn't care about family. She didn't care about friends or whether people liked her or didn't. She didn't care whether Edmund left her or joined forces with Uncle Jimmy or whether Nadia took Dmitri to Russia or Evander flew back in time to reach Svetlana and Andrew. All she cared about was the bright blue planet she called her own, its vast resources, and whether or not she would remain seated at the head of the conference table.

Evander would join forces with the other side, the side that would try to change her mind, or worse, try to stop her, and she would prepare for some attack that may or may not happen, that may or may not have anything to do with Edmund. She wanted Evander to go. That much was clear. She demanded that he go . . . and yet he still couldn't make sense of it. *Why is she pushing me out like this?*

As the Vasquezes said their final goodbye, Evander viewed the three pods set in a row for himself, Elsa, and Max, and imagined the voyage ahead. How he'd find Natasha and meet with Jimmy and Edmund, and the Moon Children . . . and all at once the answer came to him as if it had been right there from the start: Caroline believed she and her clones would fight them all—and win.

EPILOGUE

Neither Fran nor Lisa knew what to wear to the Peterman household.

Three days after Max and Evander soared out of Earth's atmosphere in a spacecraft of the kind human vision cannot detect, a dinner invitation arrived via text from Evander's wife, Nadia: 6 p.m. Her place. Casual attire. "Looking forward to seeing you both. Please come," she had written.

So they dressed in some of their better "everyday" clothing: jeans and a new black tee for Fran, a cute but not fancy dress for Lisa. On the way, they stopped for flowers and wine, as if it were just another social occasion. Never mind that neither Fran nor Lisa had spoken with Nadia in the past and knew her only as Evander's wife and the former first lady.

Martin answered the door and let them in. He even said it was nice to see them again, with his subtly robotic inflictions.

They stepped inside and lingered in the foyer for a second. Fran was almost as nervous as the first time he'd been there. Martin closed the door behind them and said, "Please follow me."

"Any messages from the travelers?" Lisa asked, and Martin said, "No, ma'am. Not yet."

Some things were different from the last time Fran had visited the Peterman household, when security had descended like locusts because Natasha had been taken. A lack of activity had replaced that atmosphere, a quiet of the sort that settles in when half the family has gone away, he supposed. Of course, a few secret service patrolled inside and out, but their presence was in no way intrusive.

He smelled something mouthwatering, like pasta with melted butter and sautéed butternut squash.

Martin led them through the kitchen, into the garden room, where Nadia, forehead creased in deep thought, first startled and then rose from the couch. It was strange to see her in ordinary jeans and a white blouse rather than the usual finery she wore as First Lady.

"Thank you for coming," she said. "I didn't hear the bell."

"Thanks for having us," Lisa said as she leaned in for a loose hug, and Fran did the same. Nadia looked about as resilient as a handkerchief.

"We brought you peonies for good fortune." Lisa handed her the bouquet. "It's so nice to meet you."

When Nadia smiled, the happiness didn't quite reach her eyes. "They are beautiful, and appropriate, too," she said with an accent like Svetlana's. Fran had always loved the way Svetlana spoke, and hearing Nadia somehow made him feel like his old friend might show up at any moment and light the room with her personality.

Martin took the flowers and wine, and left the room. Dmitri lay on his back on a blanket beyond the couch, where Natasha's toys had been the last time Fran visited. A digital screen propped on a stand had been pushed to the side wall along with the various bins of dolls and books that occupied the room's perimeter. Dmitri held his ring of keys and seemed not to notice that anyone had joined them.

"How are you doing since Max left?" Nadia asked.

"Not gonna lie," Fran said, unable to hold back a frown, "it's been tough."

Her cheeks hollowed with seriousness. "Unfortunately, I know what you mean."

"Of course you do," Lisa said, touching her arm. "How are you getting along? If there's anything we can do, please let us know."

"I'm fine," she said, shrugging, "but with just Dmitri and myself in the house, it's too quiet around here."

She seemed to want to appear "fine" but couldn't quite muster the strength.

"No worries, though," she said, in an obvious attempt to be more upbeat. "Evander will bring them all back safely. I gave him strict orders to find Natasha and come straight home."

They all chuckled out of politeness.

"I trust him completely," Fran said, using his serious voice.

"Evander is nothing if not trustworthy," Nadia said, though she didn't meet Fran's eyes when she said it.

He knew she was right, and yet her words failed to comfort him, just like they failed to comfort her. No matter Evander's honorable intentions, many things could happen: Max could come back an old man or dying of some outer-space disease or with missing limbs. Knowing Max, he'd meet up with other travelers and decide to tag along with them on a trip, wherever they were going, or, worse, never come back at all, like Svetlana's birth parents.

Of course Fran wouldn't verbalize these fears because Lisa believed this was merely the first trip in Max's new career, that he would come and go on many trips in the future, always returning home. And maybe he would.

If Max did come back, and he decided he wanted to spend his life traveling, Fran entertained the idea of him and Lisa becoming travelers as well, but as much as he might want to join Max, he couldn't see himself doing it. He had no desire to leave Earth, and being faced with the real-life possibility only reinforced the feeling that he was exactly where he was supposed to be.

The three of them sat at the coffee table and someone came in and served them drinks. It was nice, but these "normal" things didn't feel so normal anymore, not since Caroline had showed her true self to the rest of the world. The government had done its best to explain away the giant alien that appeared out of nowhere to end the Battle of Philadelphia. It was a hoax, they said. CGI. A technological trick involving light and shadow. But according to the polls several news stations had conducted, at least half the country's population chose to believe the alien's appearance marked the beginning of a new world order where aliens— not humans, clones, or hybrids—dominated.

For the past three days, only light traffic rolled along the highways and people let their dogs out in the backyard rather than taking them for walks. No lines formed at the grocery stores or the banks, post offices, and gas stations, and hundreds of thousands of people called in sick for work.

Here at home, it was as if a plague had arrived in Kirksberg. The sidewalks remained empty. The shops, closed. It was rare to see a car drive down the road. No one wanted to risk breathing the Kirksberg air, not that that made any sense. In truth, they didn't want to risk running into Caroline Jovian—or any other Jovian for that matter.

If he had to guess, Fran would say everyone was waiting for Caroline to send a message or make a statement. But she hadn't done that. No one knew what she would do next. Or even whether she was the alien or had brought one to Independence Lawn with her. Thousands of theories originated from this one event and would no doubt continue to form in the years ahead.

"How's Dmitri doing these days?" Lisa asked.

"Dmitri's fine. Of all the people on this planet, he's probably doing better than most." Nadia laughed.

Fran wasn't sure what she'd meant but figured it had to do with the fact that he seemed unconcerned by what went on outside of his own small world.

One of the kitchen help came in and called them to dinner. When they finished eating, they didn't linger at the table because Nadia said she didn't like to leave Dmitri alone for long. Apparently he rarely left the garden room. As they walked back in, a caregiver passed them with an empty plate and a spoon. Dmitri still lay on his back, jingling his keys above his head. Poor kid looked like he weighed about forty pounds.

As Lisa and Nadia sat on the couch with their coffee, discussing something about the upcoming UFO Festival and whether the town would still have it after what had happened, Fran's cell rang. He didn't recognize the number and was about to put it back in his pocket, but then he remembered the last time he didn't recognize a number and how Andrew told him to answer it and it ended up being Evander. So he tapped the button and said, "Vasquez."

He continued across the room to where Dmitri lay, and lowered into an armchair a few feet away.

"Fran, hi, it's Ida."

The voice struck him like an arrow aimed at his head. "Ida?"

"I have important information to pass on to you."

He hunched over his cell in a protective manner and whispered, "Ida Moore?"

"Yes, Ida Moore. Of course Ida Moore. What year is it that you still need to ask me that question?"

"Uh . . ."

Ida had joined forces with the Jovians decades ago, after creating the connection between NASA (her former employer) and Starbright International. At ninety-some-odd years old, she still traveled for them, which was something Fran would not have believed had he not seen her climb into one of the spaceship's pods. He'd not heard from her in fifteen years, since Svetlana left. So that would actually make her over one hun—

"Listen, I don't have time for you to get your head on straight," she snapped. "I'm calling because you're the only one I can trust. The *only* one. Do you understand?"

"Okay, but I still don't know if I trust *you*, sorry to be blunt."

"And I love you for that. You shouldn't trust me. You shouldn't trust anyone. But we know each other well, as I've told you before. In another universe, we're good friends, remember?"

"Yes, I recall you telling me that. And I'm willing to give you the benefit of the doubt only because I know how crazy the Jovian world we live in—"

"Okay, okay," she said, speaking over him, "first thing you need to do when you get off the phone is to reach out to Drew. You know who Drew is, I assume."

"The leader of the clones? I met him when Svetlana was still here. Can't say I liked him much."

"No one does," she said, "but he's important, and you need to get in touch with him."

"Fine. What's the message?"

"I don't *have* a message. He knows something, or he's

doing something, and you need to be in on it. We've come to a critical juncture. I've done all I can as an ambassador. It's not yet a dire situation, so don't panic. I wouldn't use *dire* to describe it. But you two will have to work together."

The fact that she even mentioned the word *dire* raised his blood pressure. "You know, Ida, this is the kind of phone call that's going to cause me sleepless nights for decades to come, and I already have a lot to worry about right now on a personal level."

"You're talking about Max," she said. "Listen, Max will be fine. More than fine. You've raised him well. You'll see."

Of course she would say that. Then again, maybe she knew for sure. Fran rubbed his forehead, not sure what to believe.

"Right now I need you to focus on what I'm telling you," she said loudly. "An attack on Earth is imminent, and humans and clones will have to band together whether they like it or not. So reach out to Drew, okay? It's important."

"Fine, I will," he said. "When is this attack happening, can you at least tell me that much?"

Ida didn't reply right away and Dmitri, from his blanket on the floor, made a sound wrought with strain. "S-s-s-oo-oo," followed by a strenuous grunt. Fran gazed across the room, at Nadia, who continued her conversation with Lisa without pause. He knew Dmitri could talk—he'd heard him speak before—but right now the kid wasn't facing him or anyone else, so maybe he was just . . . making sounds?

But then Dmitri spoke again: "Appen-ning-ing s-s-s-oon. That-at's what Great-gr-gr-grandmor-mor-ther s-s-said."

"Ida, I have to go," Fran said in a hurry.

No reply followed, so he checked the cell's screen: the call had already ended.

He approached Dmitri with slow caution, the way people do when attempting to pet a skittish cat.

"What else did your great-gran say?" Fran asked gently as he knelt at the edge of the blanket the boy lay on.

Dmitri rolled onto his back in a jerky way and lifted the keys, which clanged gently, like chimes. He stared into them as if they held galaxies of their own, then dropped his arm to the side and released them. He arched his back, struggling to do something.

Was he attempting to sit up?

Fran reached out to help, but needn't have. Dmitri managed a seated position on his own.

Face-to-face now, Fran gave him a serious grin when he said, "You did it. Great job, buddy."

Dmitri responded with a strange laugh that resembled consecutive hiccups. "I'ya-I'ya'am g-g-getting stronng-ger."

"I have no doubt," Fran said and sat back on his heels, observing the kid up close. Dmitri's uncanny resemblance to Svetlana once again became evident. Her rich brown hair, raised cheekbones, heart-shaped face, and blue Baltic Sea eyes. A swell of nostalgia buoyed Fran's spirit, and his dedication to Svetlana's legacy spilled like water over a dam. The feeling that it was his duty to watch over Dmitri just as Evander watched over Max became suddenly, obviously apparent.

He hoped the guys wouldn't be gone too long, but knew it could be a lifetime before he saw Max again. And now an attack was coming? How would he break it to Lisa? Maybe he wouldn't have to. After all, Evander didn't want to be away from his family. Maybe they would be back before anything bad happened on Earth.

Ida said an attack was imminent. But what did that mean exactly?

Jovians and their prophecies.

"Jovians and their prophecies," Dmitri said, his neck and head jerking unpredictably.

Wait. His mouth hadn't moved. The kid had spoken each word, clean and crisp, without any trace of struggle, but his mouth hadn't moved. And Fran hadn't spoken out loud, either. He hadn't said, "Jovians and their prophecies" out loud.

What did it mean?

Had Dmitri read Fran's mind? Had he deposited his words directly into Fran's head?

The boy dropped his chin, and his giggling hiccups returned along with the innocent, crooked smile. And then he peered up at Fran, and once again Fran felt his presence inside his mind.

"Every day I get stronger," he said.

It was the strangest thing.

Fran tried to look happy for him, but he was so startled and frightened that he couldn't control his own face. This was not normal, and as his body sounded all kinds of internal alarms, Fran did his best to appear calm.

"That's good, Dmitri," he said, wondering what it could mean. "That's really good."

THANK YOU

If you enjoyed reading *Bright Blue Planet*, Book 3 in The Jovian Universe series, please leave a rating or review on your favorite online book-selling or book-loving platform (Amazon, Bookshop.org, Goodreads, Bookbub, etc.). Leaving a review is like recommending a good book to a friend.

To receive information on Kim's new releases, including Book 4 in The Jovian Universe, you can subscribe to her email list at AuthorKimCatanzarite.com.

ACKNOWLEDGMENTS

First, I want to thank my immediate family for understanding (and accepting) my writing habit. Thank you for allowing me the time to pursue my art, to reach for my dreams, and to fulfill my creative needs. I do my best to balance all things, but you know it isn't easy, and along the way, I hope I've made you proud.

To Tricia T. LaRochelle, fellow author, editor, and friend, thank you for entering the Jovian Think Tank with me, and for making me a better writer and novelist. I'm so grateful for your contributions to my work, and for your friendship.

Thank you, Ron Skelton, Katherine Bartis, and Lisa Hopwood. You've read and proofread for me time and again, and I'm so appreciative for your feedback.

I'm also grateful to Patricia Olsen, Jacqueline Boulden, and Dave Swan for being there when I really needed your sharp eyes.

Thank you Damonza, for designing the covers for my series. I couldn't ask for better!

To my readers and supporters, you make it all worthwhile. Your kind words keep me going, raise my spirits, and brighten my world. I am forever thankful.

Lastly, thank you Mom, Dad, and Jen for giving me the solid foundation I need to feel brave enough to try.

ABOUT THE AUTHOR

Kim Catanzarite remembers looking at the moon through a telescope as a little girl growing up in Ridgewood, New Jersey, and becoming spellbound by the enormity and brightness of the sky. Today, she enjoys watching *Ancient Aliens* and readily admits that she wants to believe. She lives in South Jersey with her husband and daughter.

Made in the USA
Middletown, DE
20 September 2024